Dancing at the Colony

Cheryl Blaydon

North
Country
Press

Dancing at the Colony

Copyright © 2020 by Cheryl Blaydon

ISBN 978-1-943424-57-3

Library of Congress Control Number: 2019953598

North Country Press
Unity, Maine

Being deeply loved by someone gives you strength,
while loving someone deeply gives you courage.

Lao Tzu

Like the hem of a flirty dress, the bottom tier of a large crystal chandelier shimmered with the edge of dawn as it crept into the Colony Hotel. The time was six a.m. The warm October sun would soon burst between the opened drapery only to expose the floaty dust particles that will dance in the stale and soundless ballroom—a frieze for an artist with a fanciful soul.

Chapter 1

In her room at the Colony, Hazel Mowry pushed two gold rings over the knobs of her arthritic fingers. Long gone was the lithe ingénue who'd first set foot in Kennebunkport's landmark hotel. The digital clock said 5:18, cold blue numbers in a white plastic case, harsh against all the remembered florals. She'd dressed in black jersey, a so-called walking suit, and soft-soled shoes, which in the bathroom mirror had made her look like an aging cat burglar, though the only thing she'd steal if she was lucky, was an hour alone before the hotel came to life. John had always said the hotel had good bones, and yet had he lived, she knew he would have disparaged the reasoning for keeping the same quirky mix of colonial and bright cottagey furniture that probably dwelled in all the rooms. Or the large exquisite hooked rug—he preferred the Orientals. She could almost hear him mock-sneezing the bold blossoms that wrapped the walls until paper and window trim came together and framed the sky—still the color of secrecy. Nothing, and yet everything had changed in the years since. And now, her granddaughter slept in the adjoining room in a lesser garden of different hues. Ellis was her heart, the gift that kept on giving and the main reason Hazel was putting herself through this little dance down memory lane in the first place. She had offered to be on loan, providing moral support and her much needed checkbook; weddings here were not cheap. But right now, what Hazel needed and wanted most was some time alone downstairs in the ballroom, a chance to reclaim her own place in its wedding history. Taking the photographs out of her case, she tossed aside the plastic carrier and quietly slipped from the dizzying garden into the overnight hush of the hallway and its walls of soothing coral paint. She ran her fingertips over the ribbed wainscoting, which drew the eye to a single window that also framed what was left of the night. But then, like a poltergeist without a purpose, the image of a wedding dress hanging from a padded satin hanger in front of that same window flitted through her brain. Its silken material backlit and appearing to float. Had this scene been in one of the photographs she had left at home, she wondered, or just something buried deep in her subconscious. Or, did these 'good bones' harbor the unsettled spirit of some poor forgotten bride who'd never ended up with a wedding album in which to show it off. "No such thing as ghosts." Hazel's croakiness hung in the air. She took a good breath and said, "Ghosts begone!" The perfect acoustics for a haunting, she mused, but then as she reached the stairs, she looked back toward the middle spot where those words may have landed—just in case.

Once downstairs, it was like opening a book that had been started a hundred times but never finished. Bathed in artificial light, the large room was at once as familiar as an old theatre, the well-grouped furnishings, a supporting cast to an unannounced picture show that she also might have walked out on had she known about the ending.

Some of the chairs were slipcovered, which could account for seasonal changes, and if her memory was correct, the furniture had been rearranged to accommodate more guests, or perhaps there was just more of it. But everything, including the way her hand glided across and over the curves of the massive wood mantelpiece, or the objects it held, had a timeless quality to it. And, the entire scene was still as appealing as it had been to girls in their twenties who'd never seen anything like it.

Hazel wanted to hurry and yet she paced herself, listening for subtle nuances hiding in the quiet, letting her memory do all the work. She stood still absorbing the familiar and that which was not, especially the oils in muted greens and browns and slashed with white. Big rectangles of contemporary art painted on wrapped canvas, nakedly exposed without a gold frame to enhance the rich, dark paneling—a grouping that was disturbing in spot just crying for a Degas or a Monet or at least a huge Maine seascape.

Holding back on what even she knew to be a collector's snobbery, she kept searching for the spot that had played such an important part when recounting the memories of this hotel, a looming place she'd built up as a comforting cocoon and a place to dream, because it's where she had left so many of her own. *Or it's a place to hide the ones you must.* And suddenly, she was startled by what she hadn't forgotten.

On a crisp, October morning generations ago, a wedding party waiting to be photographed had taken over the lawn, viewed by anxious guests and relatives lingering where she now stood. The tall windows provided a clear view of the posed group backdropped by a rapidly changing fall sky and an ocean in flux. A heady excitement was in the air long before a fierce wind blew in off the water to replace high spiritedness with trepidation. Six bridesmaids' dresses ballooned outward, shielding their groomsmen who were forced upright by stiff wingtips while they all tried to keep an eye on the two flower girls with rosebuds wreathing their golden heads. They'd stood against the gusts until the wind rearranged all their hairdos and threatened to topple the little girls, who were already afraid of the swirling seagulls. By then, rose petals had been dumped like birdseed, and when everyone was herded inside, the once adorable girls turned whiny and out of control.

4

And while their overwrought mother was doing her best to calm her little ones, Hazel, rearranging her own hair, saw the hired photographer grab a mimosa from a nearby tray and down it in one gulp before reaching for a second. He turned and she blushed to see that his laser-like focus was directed squarely at her. Then she turned away, but not before he winked and ran a hand through his treacle-black hair. That was the moment the wind subsided and the sky cracked open its robin's egg blue, setting the drama right again.

Hazel's recall was so strong that her free hand reached up to touch the spot, only to be reminded of the hollows of her cheeks that she had tried unsuccessfully to ignore in the bathroom mirror.

"Another early bird, I see."

She nearly dropped the photographs, but then the male voice moved out from the thin shadow his body had created. Dressed in black—lurking like her perhaps—they made an odd pair at this foolish hour. A small grin appeared as though he was in on the joke, but instead of photographs, he held up what seemed to be an expensive digital camera.

"I prefer the sunrises," the stranger said.

"I'll leave you to it then." Any other time, Hazel's curiosity would have demanded she stay and talk, but not this morning. The corridor she was looking for was only a few yards ahead and led to the ballroom and the main reason she was wandering around pretending she knew what she was doing.

A sense of déjà vu prickled her skin. There'd been a similar walk, decades ago when she had restlessly followed the purr of office equipment and humming electrical fixtures and passed by the semi-hidden alcove just off to her left.

And beyond that, emanating from behind closed doors, the pulse of activity waiting to be awakened. *The way it was in the small hours of a very magical night.* She slowed, letting the feel of her surroundings sink in, rewinding the clock and her motive—as if any of this would make a difference to the dead.

To her right was the gift shop, dark, except for the arc of a tiny spotlight pointed at an impressive lighthouse print, the type of art she often shipped off to friends from away. An LED bulb had been left on to show off the inside of the display case. Gone it seemed, were the tourist collectables and kitschy souvenirs and replaced, perhaps by an ambitious buyer, with upscale items she didn't need. Even with the still-necessary notecards by local artists and postcards of scenic vistas, one could only use so many decorative wine stoppers and hand painted coasters or blown glass bud vases. Things she might have coveted during the period when the photos she held had been taken. Items that would by now have been lost in moving or thrown into yard sales as were so many objects saved from that era. She felt proud to have changed and become a great hurler of things no longer necessary, a lesson which could have proved helpful against any emotional fallout that over the years had actually needed to be hurled.

She kept on going. The mind plays funny tricks and maybe more so when attacked by the plaque of old age. Even if the seventies were the new sixties. Had she watered her memories down too much or, because of Sloane, let them feed on indigestible scraps of all the pent-up anger and heartbreak harbored in the years since. How much could she retrieve this weekend that would make a difference to the outcome of her own life? But as she pondered such a monumental question, her feet had already taken her across the threshold of the room that held so much promise for the girl she'd long put aside.

Hazel knew without question that if not for Ellis and her needs, she wouldn't even be here trying. Just like she knew that once upon a time, she had imagined a very different life.

The Colony was more than a grand old hotel, it was a vigilant godmother with watchful windows on the Atlantic and all who sailed her. At least, that's what Hazel's younger self had imagined when standing before it that very first time. But this time around, there was a tug and pull on her heart for very different reasons, something almost palpable about the room's atmosphere, as if time really *had* waited for her to catch up.

The photographs nearly slipped from her fingers; she'd wasted so much time fabricating reasons not to return, worrying her head off about what would happen and how she'd feel, especially in those early years of her marriage. And no matter what she'd thought or wished for or dreamed about, there had never been a proper way to prepare for such a return. This hotel might be the same, but she was not. No matter how much she had longed for those so dearly loved to be here in this room, waiting. There was no other thing to do, she realized, nothing left at all but to pretend their embrace, and wait in return.

~

They had all been so proper back then, the girls in blue taffeta, cinched into their seamed cotton bras and rubberized girdles and pointy-toed shoes with kitten heels, a scourge on women's feet once again in fashion. But they had also been coming into their own in the '60s, finding a voice in a man's world, yet still too timid to go against the grain. Traversing the tightrope of the times, and often without grace, only to see some of what they'd fought for swinging back around to hit them in the face. Like a giant pendulum gone amuck.

Chapter 2

It had been nearly a half-century, but in her mind's eye, Hazel could still pinpoint the highlights of her maid of honor's dress created by that opulent chandelier. The deeper shade of blue was, according to lore, the color of righteousness, and unbeknownst to her at the time, would set the tone for many things throughout her life. Suddenly, with a fresh eye, Hazel realized that the perceptive wedding photographer who'd made her blush like a schoolgirl, had also zeroed in on the way the light had engaged the folds of her dress, and beyond that, the way the sun had accessed the entire room on that fall morning. Those angles were absent at this hour in early spring. Today, the floor-to-ceiling drapery panels seemed to thwart the hasty shadows flung across the walls by an uncertain light. Or perhaps it was the absence of so many years creating the uncertainty. Her recall might be playing tricks, but she suddenly didn't care: *What had she hoped to find that night, poking around the hotel after everyone had gone to bed?* So many forgotten yesterdays and only one that really mattered in this moment. The one that had kept her tossing and turning all last night. Hazel shook her head —

could she reclaim the remembered music, those first, unidentifiable notes throbbing with life, luring her into this very room? Or the feeling of being so close it was as if they were sewn into an imaginary suit that would soon create intimacy the likes of which she'd never known. Without intent, her body had already done so, feigning a dance step. She stumbled—the heavy soles were not meant to glide and apparently, neither was she. To save the moment and her dignity, she moved one of the straight-back chairs toward the center of the room where the wedding photographs could come back to life, and once seated, closed her eyes. Not the ticking of a clock or the sound of her own breathing penetrated her thoughts. And then…a kaleidoscope of color unleashed by a silent motive flashed like a movie reel, the projector clicking off the tempo as the party ramped up and the bridal couple snuck away. So many moving parts, the before and after: forgotten boutonnieres, frantic mothers, rose petals underfoot, a tilting cake, laughter and music and tearful goodnights. Hearing footsteps, Hazel opened her eyes. The crowd had left her wanting more.

Chapter 3

"What on earth," Ellis asked.

It took a moment for Hazel to compose herself, but then she smiled; Ellis's raised brows carried the distinct expression Hazel often saw on John's face. In many ways, Ellis bore an uncanny likeness to her adored grandfather, even took to scavenging his old shirts to use as a cover-up when she went off in his skiff. But this morning, the very grown-up version of their granddaughter had managed to make an ordinary, thigh-length sweater, a colorful scarf, and heather-toned leggings look quite fashionable.

"I love your hair," Hazel said. Ellis had worn it down this morning, exposing the lighter blonde streaks she'd recently experimented with, along with different hairstyles to think about for her wedding day. And she was, to Hazel's delight, wearing a stylish pair of black ballet flats.

Women had come a long way from the days of ghastly girdles and other trappings of discomfort foisted on Hazel's generation. And then she remembered the lift provided beneath her jersey top, the supportive underwires giving her figure what time had taken away. *Maybe there's no justice after all*, she thought as she got up to give Ellis a hug. "Did I mention that I found the prettiest lingerie in blue to go with my new sapphire blue dress for your wedding? I thought it would be a fun homage to the girls in blue taffeta," she said, tapping one of the photographs.

Ellis had no idea why that made any difference, but then, nothing about finding her grandmother in this room at this odd hour was making any real sense. "We're going to be following in your footsteps," she said as she glanced at the photos.

"I hadn't thought about it like that," Hazel said. "I like it."

"Is that Gramps!"

"In the flesh." Hazel steered Ellis back toward the doorway and said, "I thought these might help you get an idea of what this wonderful space looks like all gussied up." She watched Ellis's expressions, looking from the photos to the real thing and back again. "Lovely, wasn't it?" Hazel said. The picture didn't quite do it justice, but John Mowry had twirled her beneath that magnificent chandelier much to the envy of Sloane, the bride and Hazel's closest friend in the world. "Even with a bum arm," said Hazel, "John swept me off my feet that day, literally. Clumsy accident or not, there wasn't anything he couldn't do, he bragged, even dance." *Those moments will be engrained for a lifetime.* Hazel's eyes beseeched the echoes in the room to speak kindly. That was the night John proposed, leaving her in the following days to mull her fate while he went back to work. They had both drunk a lot of champagne, and being a wife had its temptations in a time when being single after a certain age was a trifle unorthodox among their crowd.

A time when her friends' mothers were filling their daughter's hope chests with more than dreams, while hers remained empty. It had been more than enough to make her question everything. She surmised in the days and weeks that followed, it was also the main reason that had caused her to act out in such a reckless way once he'd gone home.

Back then, they had all talked of marriage. They never talked about lust.

"Gramps was a braggart?"

"It was how he masked his shyness, at least before he'd made a name for himself." Hazel swept the room with her arm. "Are you still sure about this? You were awfully quiet on the ride down from Boothbay."

"The room *is* pretty amazing!"

"Do I detect *but* in there somewhere?"

"I think it's more like, *is it really me?*"

"I think it suits you just fine. What does your mother think?"

"She's on board, but says since you're paying, it's really up to you."

"Your mother's a twit," Hazel said. "And you can tell her I said so."

"She's not, Gran!"

"Don't get me started. On top of her penchant for gossiping, she's now become a ditherer, and it isn't becoming."

"I'm not condoning, but I think the gossiping somehow makes her feel important."

"Important, huh? Then your father should have followed his brother up the ranks of Hannaford instead of keeping that little grocery going in Boothbay Harbor. Then you all could have lived in a seaside mansion in Scarborough."

"But we love our house."

"Then why were you so anxious to leave it?" When they all gathered, Hazel mentally framed them in a Norman Rockwell poster even though their lives had never been that idyllic. And yet, the fear of the beloved family home going to strangers had always brought out her caustic side.

"I had to or I would have stayed forever, you know that. I needed to try something new Gran, spread my wings or I'd have resented not trying."

"And I know that Walter Scott Tucker was not your

16

best choice in a husband."

"There you go again, making him sound like a clothing brand. Why don't you ever just call him Walter, like everybody else, or even dickhead."

"Ellis, really."

"Sorry."

"Well at least my way keeps me from voicing such names even though it had crossed my mind."

"I've never forgiven myself for being so stupid."

"You were never stupid, Ellis, maybe just a bit too naïve, and a little impatient."

"And inexperienced enough to believe I'd have a marriage like you or Mom instead of the angry penis I ended up with."

"Wow!"

"I just read an announcement in the *Press Herald* that his law firm has made him partner: Remy, Tandler, *and* Tucker—go figure."

"I know how much he hurt you, but honey you have to stop berating yourself, especially now with all the joy that's ahead of you."

"Then let's agree with my shrink that he was just a stepping stone, okay?"

"OKAY!"

"And, promise you'll talk with Dad when we get back."

"Linden will come around, don't worry. He just needs to flap his arms a bit right now, let his pride air out so he can enjoy your special day. It might have been cheaper if you eloped again, but that would've hurt him more than my paying for the reception. And speaking of, where are you on the countdown?"

"You wouldn't believe how stressful the change in date has become. I've got Artie taking care of everything relating to his groomsmen, and after you and I meet with the wedding planner, we'll check out locations for the photos and anything else that needs doing in the short time we're here, but I'm a wreck."

"Just breathe."

"That's what Artie says, but he's not the one having to choose all the tiny details, not that I'd trust him to anyway, but still, it's a lot on such short notice," Ellis said. "I could've waited until the original date, but this kind of summer opening doesn't come along every day."

"Think of the poor girl who lost all her money when she canceled."

"How humiliating, you mean."

"The whole idea of a groom running off with one of the bridesmaids sounds way too cliché."

"According to our wedding planner, it happens more often than you'd think."

"Lara's seems lovely, but don't you think sharing that

kind of gossip could be bad for business."

"Nah, seems people eat that stuff up, as long as the problems belong to someone else." Ellis said. "When I told Jeanie, she told me the guy was lucky not to have his legs broken; the bride's Italian."

"You and your movies," Hazel said. "But how are the Anthonys; I haven't seen them in ages."

"Mrs. Anthony offered to put together those little net bags of almonds, which was really sweet of her, and then Mr. Anthony said we should play a tarantella, and then Jeanie came to my rescue."

"I respect anyone who likes to hang onto their heritage; after all, look at all of our clan clinging to the soil and digging up our roots."

"You know, Gran, sometimes you just amaze me," Ellis said. Silently, she worried her grandmother had gotten wind of the family tree she'd been working on before the crunch of the new wedding date.

"Sometimes I amaze myself. And now, since you're dressed, why don't you go see what's for breakfast while I go back to my room and change?"

"What's wrong with that outfit?"

"You know me better than that," Hazel said as they made their way back down the long hallway.

"As a matter of fact, I do, but who knows, this morning might have been an exception."

19

Hazel wanted to be witty and upbeat, the persona she'd adopted for her family's sake after John died, anything to keep them all from worrying about her. But it was too darned early in the morning, and if she was being honest with herself, it was more than that. Just for a few moments longer, she wanted to be *that* girl in the ballroom and not just Gran. To again experience the heightened senses that used to make her blush—love was messy by the way, and buried guilt hurt like hell, and weddings were both beautiful and sad, especially when you find out you have the wrong partner. Then she wondered whether she was thinking of Sloane or herself.

Had the circumstances been different, she might have shared more of her feelings with Ellis, but John had been placed on a high pedestal. And particularly now with just months away from her own marriage, there was no reason for Ellis to know the difficulties that came with building his career and how much Hazel had sacrificed on his behalf. Or that by the time he died, she had already dipped her hands into every available font on Sloane's behalf, praying her disease away, and for many years after, praying away the release of her own grief and anger. And that by then, Hazel hadn't been able to find words to ease the shocking discovery of her husband's sleep-like body already cold to the touch, gone before his time. Although when was there ever a right time. But it was that final loss, and her inability to fathom more prayer, which had pushed her to seek solace in a compilation of beautifully written and illustrated books on Buddhism.

In the end, even those had grown dusty on her bedside table until she'd moved her loneliness to another location.

Sloane used to tease her, calling her a noble agnostic because Hazel liked to hedge her bets by making an appearance in the town's many churches even though none of Hazel's family had been particularly religious. But Sloane had been better at prayer, and still none of it worked. She was far better at forgiveness too, especially when it came to the turmoil unnecessarily created over treatment plans and the ensuing issues with her husband.

And now, Hazel reflected, there'd been a half century of missed opportunities in which to summon the ghosts, toss the mental junk, and especially to forgive, and this fact was beginning to poke her where it hurt. Hardest of all, because coming back to the hotel had opened that door as well, she had to try to find a way to also forgive herself.

She'd put it all down on paper during those rapidly changing days when Sloane was ill, when only journaling helped save Hazel's sanity. The words she used to recite until it no longer mattered, and then she tucked them away in her desk and each year on the anniversary of Sloane's death, she tried to assuage the pain by reading those words all over again, though nothing had ever worked.

All of a sudden, Hazel was dizzy with thinking. A slight nag at her temples was an indication of what could come from carrying around a bag full of secrets. She could almost feel their weight slowing her down, and she realized Ellis was staring at her.

"You okay, Gran?" Ellis linked her arm through Hazel's, spurring her on.

"I will be, as soon as I get a little food in me." Hazel wasn't exactly sure what she needed and she wouldn't have been able to articulate it anyway, not to Ellis, but she was warmed by Ellis's sweet out-of-the-blue possessiveness. But the gesture seemed to fall on top of the other things Hazel hadn't dealt with very well; she needed to try harder with her daughter. Janet, her raven-haired girl whose dismay often shone through mink-colored eyes, was somehow always out of sync with the rest of the family, and now in her fifties, she was far less sensitive to others than Ellis. But then again, divulging secrets to Janet after so many years of guarding them, would be like watching her as a little girl picking scabs off her knees — there would be scars!

"Looks like it's still too early for breakfast," Ellis said waving her free arm toward the glassed-in "Porch" with all the empty tables. "I can think of a couple of names I would have chosen for that area even if it is a porch."

"Maybe they have a suggestion box somewhere," Hazel said looking out at the water, which had gone from charcoal to a dove gray. "May and October, bookends to the long harsh winters."

"The gloom is getting you down, Gran, I can tell."

"Maybe so, but you, young lady can concentrate on your walk down the aisle come summer," Hazel said as she unlinked her arm from Ellis's.

"I guess no one else gets up this early."

"Looks like we're it," Hazel said. "But forgive me if I'm not ready to have that weather talk with all those first-time-to-Maine visitors."

"Curmudgeon."

"Not. More like set in my ways. Do you know how many times I get asked 'what do you do here all winter'?"

"We do talk a lot about the weather, Gran, even you, but I'd be happy to run into another prospective bride, just to exchange ideas about all this stuff," Ellis said patting her tote.

Hazel tilted her head, "Hear that? Behind the partition."

"I hope that's the breakfast crew; I'm dying for a cup of good strong coffee."

The sound carried: shuffling feet, the clink of silverware and china, muted instructions from a faceless waitstaff running through their morning prep. And as she urged Ellis forward, the noise turned into an age-old symphony by the sudden off-key intrusion of gull song filtering in through the closest open doorway.

"I guess I'll just wait down here since I don't need to change *my* clothes!" Ellis said with a wink.

Hazel put a hand on Ellis's back, laughing at her impertinence and said, "Now shoo, there's a nice big chair over there in the great room with your name on it where you can sort out your *stuff*." Beyond the room, the sea was still in cahoots with the drab sky, defying definition and promising nothing, and Hazel wondered about the man in black as she walked up the stairs. It could hardly be the right morning for a sunrise-seeking photographer.

As she approached her room, muffled voices behind closed doors and the gurgle of water through pipes filtered into the hall. *Maybe someone for Ellis to commiserate with after all.* Then a door slammed on the floor above at the same time Hazel opened hers, only to be met with a scene reminiscent of a *Harlequin* romance, and ignored earlier in her haste to get downstairs. As though left by hurried lovers, the crumpled white coverlet lay exhausted across the bed, and her Moroccan dressing gown looked just as weary with its sleeve caught on the edge of a small chair where Hazel had flung it. On top of the bed, her overnight bag yawned open in disapproval. She found her bottled water and took an aspirin for good measure and her eyes fixed on the bizarre way in which she'd left her things, and she caved to a sudden need to lie down. Checking the clock, and not bothering with the bed's appearance, she removed her shoes and stretched out. *Just for a few minutes, that's all.* But that thought was soon joined by thoughts of Sloane as they bumped against the ones of John, until she fell asleep.

Chapter 4

Hazel's scream brought her head off the pillow with a start. She glanced at the clock. She hadn't been out long, but she was certain the visuals would linger: a ripped blue dress, crystals falling from a chandelier, broken glass and blood everywhere. Vivid and ugly and not the first time either, and she couldn't get out of the black outfit fast enough. A second and never-worn outfit was hanging on the back of the door, and even though the wrinkles had shaken out during the overnight hours, the material seemed to hang listlessly and looked almost as bereft as her face appeared in the mirror. Staring down the discomforting reflection, she lifted her chin against the tide of her own opinion and splashed cold water on her face, willing away the terrible images. But could she, really? The worst of them might have been buried—the news item pushed to page six to spare the family—but they existed, dredged up and swirling around like it was 1984 all over again. And though Ellis was waiting, food was now the least of Hazel's concerns. She noticed the slight tremor in her hand as she replaced the towel on a nearby hook. Ellis had a keen eye, Hazel thought as she grabbed for her peony-scented moisturizer—the one that graced the face of an aging star bearing no resemblance whatsoever to her own—to cover the small brown spots that in the past few years had shown up like mildew on parchment. Flaws Sloane would never know. Would Sloane have lived long enough to despise getting old, or would she, like everything else thrown at her, simply deal with it: eye tucks, brow lifts, vaginal creams and all the rest that allowed for a youthful redux? *If only.* On her special day, Sloane had epitomized everything about the hotel's eloquence and style, walking out in the purest white velveteen and silk—befitting the time of year as well as the money from her father's insurance policy, which happened to be the only thing he'd ever done right. And now, the only consolation was that Sloane would remain forever young. Hazel blinked away a threatening tear. They'd been best friends since fourth grade, the only skinny blondes in a sea of wholesome pony-tailed brunettes, and had grown up confident in the fact that they knew everything about each other. They'd been just as arrogant about the world they would enter as adults. But they emerged as two very different individuals: Sloane, sleek and fashionable and hungry for love almost to the point of promiscuity, while Hazel had been cautious to a fault, righteous some might have said, at least until the night of Sloane's wedding. Still, their friendship had remained solid, unshakable even in the midst of the near-tectonic shifts perpetrated by others. Up until Sloane married Mike Kaplan on that fall day in 1963. And Hazel had been right, he *was* the last man to ever disappoint her friend. *Smile or you'll cry,* Hazel thought leaning in close to the mirror. Her lips, like the rest of her face, had succumbed to a network of fine lines. *What next?* John had always said she needn't worry; he would love her no matter what. And for a long while after, Hazel cared little about her looks. That was then. Reaching for the last tube she owned of a sold-out brand of lipstick in a rose pink, she blotted lip against lip, a universal act performed every day by women she'd never meet. She made a last adjustment to her hair and moved slightly away from the mirror—her mother's face peered back. Midge, at a similar age but hair whiter without the blonde shade now in vogue for senior women—a face well lined and somber. Still, the resemblance was unmistakable. Hazel had long made peace with the idea that a mother who'd preferred being called by her first name, had also more than likely caused much of her own somberness, having made her marital bed with the tall, handsome though uneducated farmhand without thinking it through. Not that it mattered after he'd gone. Once they'd moved closer to town—the year Hazel turned fourteen—her father had walked off. Left without a trace and her mother seemed not to mind, continuing to hold her head up against what she had called 'a shitload of gossip by too many churchgoers'. Especially, Hazel recalled, on those cold winter days when Midge swirled a little of Allen's Coffee Brandy into her morning cup—a proper Maine toddy she liked to say. Life had been hard back then, not only for them, but for all their friends and neighbors. Fortunately, Aunt Charlotte who was both a teetotaler and a spinster, had stepped up and Hazel was given a good state college education, which she basically squandered by getting married right away. And, because in those days, men could be heard saying that young wives could become like their mothers as they aged, Hazel took to being a little more like Mother Mowry: strong, sure, and very well groomed.

Hazel promptly turned and walked out of the bathroom with her shoulders back and her bag of superficial flaws tucked under her inherited chin, willing away whatever Ellis might pick up on. *There's a lot of life in you yet.* Hazel stopped abruptly, allowing the innocuous phrase to peel away another layer of aging angst until the words sounded like a distant cheer from the crowd in a place where it all began. Her energy took a new direction. Though she did resist the urge to let her body take sway over common sense. *Foolish dance steps could become a habit,* she thought just as the new and rather thin jacket swung away from her hips. Perhaps the lightweight brocade wasn't the best material for a stingy spring morning near the water. A plumpish, rather overzealous saleslady where she'd bought the designer outfit had been quite free with her compliments, but Hazel had been doomed anyway by the inability to resist the perfect color (blue) and so she'd ignored the obvious.

She buttoned the last button, and pushing aside the clumsy walking shoes slipped into her copycat pair of black flats, and all but glided to the window. And, of course, the questionable sky had changed again, unfolding in layers, indecisive—the color of turmoil. *Someone's walking over a grave,* Midge used to say whenever she felt a shiver in her old bones.

But unlike Hazel, Midge had never become comfortable around water, had not even entertained going for a sail when her much-loved son-in-law had offered to take her out in the bay.

Hazel cupped her hands on the window pane searching the dark for an ocean she knew would still be frigid with winter's last breath, taunting like it always did this time of year. She shivered. The older she got, the more she mourned the hardy northerner she'd once been—just her boiled wool jacket and good gloves for whatever needed doing, not even a hat to protect her wavy blonde hair.

But as she stood before the window in this telling place, and even more, she mourned the friend with whom she had shared so much.

Chapter 5

Downstairs in the large open space where Hazel had left her, Ellis waited, like a little girl playing grown-up, her slender frame getting lost in the oversized wing chair, and like a child, she couldn't stop fidgeting. She hated waiting, even though she was used to her grandmother's obsession with looking properly turned out. But her discomfort this morning was in part because there wasn't anyone to talk to, no other soon-to-be brides in similar situations with whom she could commiserate about details and timing and photographers. And it would be a couple of hours before their scheduled meeting with the wedding planner. *Face it, you're a bundle of nerves.* And she was allowing them to run her over this morning, and how nice it would be to have even a disgruntled tourist or two to talk with, someone she could make feel better about the slow crawl of traffic this time of year and the realization that you couldn't always get there from here because of the long peninsulas that looked so close together on the map. As long as conversations didn't lead to whether or not lobsters felt pain because there was no having that discussion at all. *Curmudgeonly like Gran?* Probably, but it was a moot point since there wasn't anyone around anyway. She texted Artie to keep from talking to herself, filling him in on the minutia, missing him. She texted her dad. He was better at texting than her mother. And in between the finger-tapped words was the underlying issue that her new wedding date had interrupted the work she'd undertaken before a second marriage had even been an option. So, in fact, guilt was most likely also playing a small role in her anxiety. Modernizing Berman's hometown family market into a much trendier provisions store had initially required enough time and attention to soften the blemish Walter had left on her soul. And later, provided her with a sense of achievement and a new skill. Like learning to like herself again, both of which might not have happened if her best friend Jeanie hadn't convinced her to come back home and start over. In hindsight and very hard to fathom, it was a stinking crazy, unsuccessful, re-orbit into online dating that had paved the way for the relationship she now treasured. It had taken her more than a year to dissect her failed marriage and then another six months to realize there were men out there with whom she might be worse off: men with fake photos who were possibly hiding more than their identity; the nut case with bad breath and a penchant for daily marijuana; or the last one, a serial dater who streamed his dates' faces as his screen saver for amusement. Then, as if the gods had been downright pissed at Jeanie for encouraging such a futile exercise, Ellis met Artie while jogging the road near Barret Park.

Now that she'd learned more of her grandmother's backstory, the parallels were quite striking: they both had friendships they'd carried their whole lives. Ellis was living with someone who also culled beauty from dreams and unexpected ideas, and the Colony brought both important weddings into play. But Ellis also knew that in between the lines of unspoken words, there was far more to her grandmother's situation. *What would grandad think,* Ellis wondered as she listened to the faint moan of the wind. One of the hotel employees had just opened another door and was in the process of cranking the lower windows to bring in the awesome brininess of the sea. *If only that could be bottled.* She breathed it in while she listened to the cry of hungry gulls, and began to feel a semblance of her old self.

But she still craved coffee. And then, as if she'd telepathically signaled, a busboy appeared out of nowhere, hefting one of those giant gray bins on an awfully bony shoulder. She jumped up without thinking and banged her elbow against the odd curve of the chair. She caught up to him, following without a word and then startling him as he rested the tray of mugs and stacked them in twos next to a setup of three stainless urns and the accompanying sugar, sweetener and cream. Even before he'd finished laying everything out, she'd filled a cup and emptied two packets of sugar without realizing what she'd done. *And there goes the effort.* But she nearly swooned at the delicious sweetness until she thought of the soon-to-be challenge at this very same table: high-caloric dishes set out temptingly as part of the standard breakfast buffet, tantalizing in full color on the hotel website. *Calories or carbs,* she thought as she headed back to where she'd left her things, carefully sipping as she walked.

Daylight was finally breaking through the gray, exposing a rumpled sea as well as a man who hadn't been there before as he walked toward the wall of windows until he was directly in line with her chair. He carried a tripod and camera bag, and every few feet, he held up what might have been a light meter. *We're so screwed if we don't find a photographer soon,* she thought as she kept him in sight. Her grandmother's photos had inspired her, but she needed to find the elusive theme to pull everything together. She quickly texted Artie intending to vent while she could. There was so much to be considered. Her phone rang within seconds.

"Hey you," she answered.

"You okay; your text sounded scattered."

"I'm a bit overwhelmed, that's all."

"You can handle it babe, I know you."

"Then tell me what kind of flowers or round or square tables or what sort of gifts we should give to our guests that are portable and easy on the wallet."

"Whoa, that's an awful lot before I've even had breakfast...and yes, I'm having the full sat-fat version while I still have a chance."

"Let's not go there; I haven't eaten yet." Ellis could see the stovetop awash in spattered bacon grease and knew he'd probably make his childhood favorite: a peanut butter, banana and bacon sandwich. "What else might you be doing while I'm away?" She pictured his solid body, the fine bluish stubble darkening his jawline, his direct, hazel eyes, and she missed him even more.

"Just railing on the appliances, and I know this isn't the time to think about spending money on new, but damn, this stuff is really junk."

"Maybe if you ask nicely, the landlord might change them out; after all, we're going to be there awhile."

"Speaking of, I went through some of those drawings of John's you had stored in the blanket chest, and I think I found the right house, for when we can afford it, naturally."

"I think I'm going to cry if we have that conversation right now; it'll be something to look forward to when I get home." Ellis noticed the stranger walking away. "Sorry, I've gotta run and see if I can catch up to a photographer."

"Where'd you find someone at this hour."

"He's taking pictures around the grounds, and since I don't have anything better to do while I wait for Gran, it seems like a good idea."

"Is he good looking?"

"I'll never tell."

"You're too much."

"I'll take that as a compliment?"

"Just remember what I said—no strange men."

She heard what could easily have been mistaken for a cough if she wasn't so used to the soft rumble that came up from his chest and spilled into the line just as it went dead. He was always there when nothing else could save her from herself. It would have made her grandfather enormously proud to know what Artie was up to. *Oh, Gramps,* she thought, missing him more than ever. He was her knight who made fairy tales out of fairy houses and taught her about color-coded lobster buoys and building small cairns on rocky boulders. Rangy, and ruddy-faced— her very own superhero who'd loved the sea with a passion, and had fallen ill and with the same efficiency with which he'd handled everything. No drawn-out tests and hospital stay, just his final sleep in his favorite chair after a successful round of golf, and still wearing his lucky hat.

And then it was Gran to worry about, busying herself

with all and sundry. Hazel, queen of her domain, might be considered a tough old broad, but Ellis was far from convinced. And less so, after having seen the way her grandmother appeared earlier this morning.

And though she kept gathering it back up, Ellis's confidence still managed to slip into the what ifs, and a lot of that had a lot to do with the fact that she hadn't had to go through any of the machinations of wedding protocol the first time around. But now, sitting alone, she had allowed herself to second-guess just about everything. Was this venue too over-the-top for a second marriage? Was it a foolish waste of Gran's money? Ellis knew there were many spots closer to home around Boothbay Harbor that could provide the same overall ambiance: Ocean Point, or Spruce Point, or more to the point, the lawn at the old New Englander, which was the house Gran had deeded to Ellis's parents after Gramps died. The house was her father's choice and seconded by Artie. It was where Ellis and her brother had spent half their childhood, and a family legacy that one day would pass to Jake. She and Jeanie had devoted way too many hours weighing all the options for a wedding venue: the right destination, the perfect wedding planner, style and luster, all of it in order to get everything right this time. And not just for her mother's sake because she'd missed all the hoopla when

Ellis had eloped. She sat upright and sloshed her coffee; she needed to call Jeanie.

"I almost forgot about your fitting," Ellis said the moment Jeanie answered.

"It's all good here, but something in your voice says you're not."

"Too much time on my hands this morning. I'm waiting on Gran, as always, and still figuring out how to have the wedding of our dreams without it looking like everybody else's."

"Just remember...no walking barefoot on rocks while you wait for the wind to swoosh your veil at the perfect moment."

"And no dogs wearing fancy collars to carry the rings," Ellis laughingly shouted into the phone and then looked around sheepishly.

"Boy, are you wound up...too much coffee?"

"Only a cup, but you know me."

"Don't be one of those TV bridezillas, 'cause I may never forgive you."

Ellis realized she was getting close, but she said, "No way, but I wondered what you'd think about us lip-syncing our vows to some popular song."

"Oh, god, Artie Granger is not going to fall for that one!"

"Me neither, but I'm trying to relax. Here I am, surrounded by everything we found while we were glued to our computers, all that documented perfection, and I'm still at a loss to come up with originality."

"Ellis, listen to me, you're just stressed because of the new date, but it'll all work out, I promise."

"I can't stop thinking about that poor bride, and all that wasted money, and how it was easier to elope, but then I would have disappointed so many people, again."

"Including yourself; you and Artie deserve a nice wedding, and you're in the right place and you know it."

"By the way, we aren't the only girls in blue who'll become part of the hotel's history. Gran's best friend used the same theme fifty years ago."

"What'd they look like?"

"Nothing like ours. It was a simple design stopping just below the knee with a bell-shaped skirt, and probably made right there in the harbor, which reminds me, is Chloe's dress going to work with her expanding waistline?"

"Not much we can do about the baby bump, but to be honest, she's the only one ticked off about the change in dates."

"I'll call her when I get back."

"Is there anything else before I get in the shower. It's

Mom and Dad's anniversary and they're starting the day with a Mass."

"Give them our love." Ellis had gone with Jeanie once before and knew the family would be lined up in a front-row pew where the Anthonys always sat. Jeanie, with her expressive green eyes and Roman nose—that in profile, was identical to her father's—greeting friends in nearby pews. And when taking Communion, the way the lights caught her glossy brown hair that glistened in the sun with red highlights she'd inherited from Mrs. Anthony who sort of resembled an Italian movie star from another era.

"I will, and are you still stopping off in Portland on your way home for your fitting?"

"Scheduled for late morning on Monday. It's a chance for Gran to see it in person, and then I only have one more fitting before the wedding."

"Call me when you get back then, okay?"

"Will do, and thanks for being the best maid of honor ever."

"My pleasure, and when I finally land the guy of my dreams, you'll get to pay me back."

Ellis hung up wishing she could make Jeanie's wish come true, but so far, the best man was playing hard to get. And now, with nothing better to do, Ellis took a pen and paper from her tote; it was always best to jot things down for her mother who didn't appreciate the use of a smartphone for the important details and maybe not even the unimportant ones. When she finished, Ellis stood up, which ironically coincided with the timing of a fat herring gull about to drop in for a landing, his big yellow beak pinching what looked like a clam shell. She stayed still until his webbed feet touched down on the gazebo roof overlooking the pool and didn't move a muscle as he deftly dropped the shell. Even so, he turned his beady eye in her direction. Had he seen her or just his own reflection, there was no way to know, but he turned his head away and raised his wings, propelling his chunky body upward to catch the thermals—a far-away place her grandfather had made sound magical to a little girl with a big imagination. A lump formed in her throat, but she kept her eyes locked on the gull until all that was left was a thin scratch, like a wobbly M, shaking at the heavens. Everything would be okay no matter what. She was marrying a man much like her hero, *and* the absolute antithesis of Walter Scott Tucker.

She took in a long breath and held it for seven beats before letting go, and repeated the cycle two more times. She'd learned the technique in a yoga class years ago, and it always worked. She checked the time and considered ringing her grandmother's room, then changed her mind. Primping was just Gran's thing. Instead Ellis began to visualize her wedding day, the way she would have wanted her grandfather to see it. And the way it would look when her father got to walk her down the aisle at last. There was much to be grateful for, even if her to-do list was pockmarked with corrections and her mother was unable to cope with her hot flashes. *Footsteps.* She turned to look. A flash of color—matching tee shirts and caps and neon-bordered running shoes, and the couple was gone before she was able to put a smile on her face. She caught a glimpse of them as they peeked into the breakfast room, but then they were across the lobby and out the front door before she could acknowledge their presence. *So much for some company.* "Oh, hell!", she said as she gathered up her things. She could at least get a table.

The "Porch", a name that nudged her like a stich in her side. She really would have to find a suggestion box somewhere, she thought as she looked at the bank of windows with a great view that she knew was still hiding out there somewhere. Dropping her tote bag down on the dark wood surface of one of the smaller tables, she pulled out the chair facing the water and then put her phone next to her place setting. She was about to email the bridal salon in Portland to confirm her appointment when she heard the squeak of rubber soles.

"You've got bride-to-be written all over you."

"You peeked," Ellis said as she patted the hotel-sponsored wedding brochures. Yearning was obvious on the young waitress's face, and as she stared wide-eyed at Ellis's ring, Ellis stole a glance at the square nametag on her blouse. "And you, Sherry, have, 'I can't wait' written all over you."

"I'm just waiting for him to propose, and I wouldn't mind a ring like that."

Ellis wriggled her third finger; Artie had been very generous.

"It's wicked gorgeous."

"I think so too," Ellis said. "And it looks like your cohort over there will need a look as well."

"That's Mary; she's already a grandmother, but she does love weddings!"

"We're booked here for the last week in August, so I have my work cut out for me."

"Oh, you're the one who lucked out. You didn't hear it from me, but they're still talking about that SOB and what he did. But I'm happy for you," Sherry said just as a door off the veranda banged in the way only a guy would do. Mary let out a huge guffaw, and Ellis's head snapped sideways in time to see the waitress caught up in a mighty hug that seemed improbable coming from such an extremely thin man. "Don't mind Peter; he acts like he owns the place, but that's just because he's our most popular wedding photographer."

This guy shouldn't wear black. Ellis had spent too long

45

with someone who would have spray-tanned his face rather than let anyone see him with sallow skin hanging onto such a lean face the way Peter's looked, especially in this lighting. But then, Walter was an ass-kisser, always trying to impress, which she knew from the newspaper article, had finally paid off.

Just then, Peter took off his hat and swiped his hand over thinning hair, adding another question mark to what Ellis was beginning to think of as his affliction. This too made her think of Walter, not because he'd ever been seriously ill, but he'd vowed he'd get hair plugs if he ever began to lose his hair. What had been wrong with her, she wondered just as Peter pushed his cap further back on his head and caught her staring. Then, he winked.

Even before she had time to be embarrassed, he'd refilled a travel mug and banged back out of the same door.

"I guess I missed my chance to meet him."

"We keep his cards at the counter, just in case he doesn't come back in before you're finished. He loves the early mornings, even on days like this."

Ellis stood up to follow her, and then Mary came over and Ellis held her left hand out for inspection. "Wow," Mary said, and then, lifting her chin toward the door, "He's more like his old self this morning."

"Is he ill?" Ellis asked.

"Recuperating's more like it," Sherry answered. "Here's his card."

Ellis looked at it, and pulled out her phone to follow the link to his website: PeterHamilton.com, and said, "Thank you—it would be a blessing if I finally found my photographer."

"Are you having breakfast?"

"As soon as my grandmother comes down." Ellis went back to her table hoping that either Peter or her grandmother would return soon, all the while realizing her hoping wouldn't make her grandmother move any faster when it came to her appearance. She was known for being quite persnickety about what she wore, among other things. But there was one occasion when her grandmother had been less the matriarch of their family and more of the carefree spirit Ellis guessed enjoyed hiding in the guise of a tough New Englander.

It had been a day that Ellis knew would always stay in her memory because it was the first time she'd been taken on a tour of the original Beane homestead—an obscure property in the woods of Somerset County, and her grandmother had dressed for the outing in a pair of white jeans, a crisp chambray shirt, and tennis shoes that looked to be right out of the box. She had laughed at the way the wildflowers clung to her legs in the overgrowth that surrounded the meager country house, and had overlooked Ellis's need to wipe away the smeared glass and pry into the grimy existence that had once been a home.

The day had been finalized at the family burial plots, solidifying an idea Ellis had for a family tree, which she'd only just begun before the wedding date had been fast-forwarded. When finalized, it was to be a surprise thank you gift for her grandmother's generosity.

Ellis's stomach suddenly growled, which she was certain was caused by the intoxicating aroma of butter, sugar and fruit hot out of an oven in a kitchen she couldn't see.

A memory flashed of her childhood elbow-deep in flour. Her mouth watered in anticipation of what she would order. And her mind flew all the way back home to Boothbay Harbor and the old fashioned eat-in kitchen that her mother had coveted long before it had become her own.

All that baking that had become a plague on her mother's waistline while her dad, who preferred savory to sweet, never gained. There was a lesson somewhere in there though Ellis couldn't fathom quite where, but she was positive that the scales for men and women were unfairly balanced when it came to weight loss.

But their old house would always represent sweet memories and many of them having nothing to do with food. It was an intown treasure with a large veranda, a picture window and a wide, lush lawn meant for croquet-playing. It wasn't old enough to be considered historic, but it had been kept in its original state by her grandfather who could hammer and nail as well as he did everything else. Of course, after he died, some of that high maintenance had to be farmed out since her father's interest had always been in sales. And, whittling of all things. Ellis thought how her mother accused him of whittling away time when he could have been building their bank account, but he never minded. He was a laid-back soul, not given to drama or upward mobility. *Unlike poor Mom*, she thought. Her mother often seemed in desperate need to have what she'd missed, not only because of Ellis's elopement, but what she had also missed out on by eschewing the Mowry status to save the Berman status quo.

If she tried hard enough, Ellis could conjure all manner of things having to do with pride, but all roads led back to the harbor and the home she and Artie had made for themselves out of a plain, two-story rental with a small deck and tiny view of the water and within walking distance of Barret Park. And on this not very pretty morning, she was beginning to experience an epiphany of sorts: it mattered less what theme she'd pick—besides all that blue, and more about learning from what had been

49

missing the first time around. There were no guarantees other than a faith in each other here and now, and instead of second guessing, she thought, maybe it might be better to just be grateful for second chances.

Chapter 6

In actuality, the great room was really only a big blank canvas, Hazel thought as she looked around for Ellis. Guests could paint their own scenarios to suit their needs, no matter whether for a wedding or just a prolonged visit to Maine. Magic making, which must have been what Sloane and the entire bridal party had thought when they first arrived here so many years ago. It was obvious that no one else had come down for breakfast yet, and there was no one at the desk, though there was a bell and a tucked away office that she also remembered. It was simply too early to worry about things like that now, but she did smell coffee and something baked that had probably lured her granddaughter to the "Porch". Just as Hazel reached the wall that would keep her hidden from view, she spotted Ellis, and even without a mirror, Hazel felt her own expression softening. From a distance, she could tell that Ellis was glowing and animated as she showed off her ring to one waitress with the other one craning her neck to get a glimpse. *Perfect timing.* Hazel stepped away, moving in the direction of the one place that would offer a reprieve from the demon nightmare; she'd barely gotten a taste of the remembered joy before

Ellis had found her in the ballroom. Rounding the corner, Hazel followed the twists and turns she'd taken earlier, but this time her pulse quickened for another reason. Then, out of nowhere, she heard the unmistakable drone of a professional vacuum cleaner. "Hah!" Hoovering had been one of Midge's favorite pastimes—therapy she'd said— cheaper too. Between the Allen's and the cleaning, her mother had managed to handle many of her own disappointments quite well. But there wasn't any point being in there with the cleaners, Hazel thought as she turned around to join Ellis, and then there was silence, as if someone yanked the plug. A minute later, a loud varoom filled that silence even as the noise was redirected toward the anterooms beyond the ballroom. Hazel was poised between going forward and turning back, caught between expectation—which could be a bitch—or disappointment, which had to be made friends with no matter what. Now she knew without a doubt that Midge's views on life had begun to coalesce with her own. *All part of aging,* she thought and then as she continued down the hallway, she made a mental note to run that by Millie for good measure. By the time Hazel reached the doorway, the room had been vacated, the overhead lights turned off, even the chair she'd moved earlier returned to its rightful place along the side wall. And, for the second time within hours, she was standing on the threshold looking in at her memories, only this time she was filled with gratitude for not having chosen to stay away.

Walking to the nearby credenza, she put a manicured hand flat on its surface, perhaps in the same spot where the 8-track player had been placed—next to the rumpled jacket and a large Polaroid professional camera. There had been multiple weddings on that long-ago weekend so their photographer's presence in this room had not been remarkable, though the rest of the night certainly was. And since she had now replaced the rubber-soled shoes with smooth ones, and because no one was there to see, she tried small, tentative steps, fixing a tempo to match her unyielding joints, remembering even more. *Eduardo. Sensuous.* A word foreign to her vocabulary until by the end of the music—*Verano Porteno*—it wasn't. *Wide shoulders and untucked white shirt covering slim hips, and even without his camera lens, he'd seen her in a different light—perhaps the way he had over the rim of a champagne flute.* In the end, she'd walked into Eduardo's vision so blatantly offered and allowed it to lure her into an embrace. After so many years of learning to forget, she'd now come face to face with their reality, and she still couldn't put a name to her behavior: the lack of common sense and caution thrown to the wind; a champagne fugue, curiosity; a tempting of fate after a day full of delights and wishful thinking. Whatever it had been, this room would extract it from her one way or another, of that she was certain. Even the way he'd said her name, drawing it out with his soft accent as if it were the beginning of a song and not the hard-edged name she'd inherited. Great-grandmother Olive H, as she was referred to in the family Bible, set the tone for a multitude of grim-faced females in their line named Olive, and all given different middle names to chew over. But it was Olive H, a deceivingly frail looking woman with tied-back hair, who carried a knife at the waist of her plain, long cotton skirt. That ancestor.

And the way he'd talked — *the way of his ancestors* — he'd said as he held her unsuspecting body. *The way of the dance.* It was all there in the history he'd claimed with the assurance of any good instructor to his pupil. The palpable rhythms waking the pampas from their dusty past once all the other European dances had had their way with Argentina. The undistinguished port that she'd later read out of need as well as curiosity, had become the Paris of South America: Buenos Aires. The dance that had begun as a habanera and traveled from Cuba to tell its story: the tango.

Then, like a remarkable vintage montage reborn, years slipped away as easily as the blue silk scarf which had fallen from her once smooth neckline.

It was a few moments before Hazel could compose herself. The word earthy came to mind, another one she wouldn't have recognized in her youth. Except it had suddenly become rooted in a heat she might have ignored but for the tingling in her old-lady limbs. How could it not?

She thought of her granddaughter waiting all this time. Hazel wondered what she could possibly say without divulging intimacies she'd barely understood herself? What appeasement could she verbalize when all she wanted was to possess the precious moments that she never imagined would ever come back to thrill and most probably haunt her from here on in. Or how could she dare voice the name she'd only just become reacquainted with—*Eduardo*. And, without recognizing why, she was suddenly homesick for a place she'd never been.

"Pull yourself together," Hazel whispered into the air. Even if he were still alive and still dancing with however many women, he was as lost to her as John. She made her way to the first-floor restroom and checked her coloring. The heat was still on her face; the blush he'd always been capable of extracting from her. *Change the narrative. Change the expectation and what do you have? Freedom.* She heard the word tapping like a faint drumbeat against her heart. *Foolish*, she thought; it would take more than freedom to pursue an accidental falling-in-love a lifetime ago; it would take tons of courage and it was more than likely she was tapped out in that department too.

Instead, she fixed a smile, straightened her jacket and walked out to join Ellis for breakfast.

Chapter 7

"There you are. I was just about to go hunting for you," Ellis said.

"Sorry, I didn't expect to doze off, and besides I saw you were happily occupied or I wouldn't have left you so long."

"I think I've found my photographer, but then he disappeared and came back again, but you were obviously primping, because just look at you."

"Tease all you want, but I needed that little catnap, and then just one more peek into the ballroom."

"Are you okay?"

"Just a little field trip through my past sweetheart, nothing to worry about." Trampling over an emotional mine field was more like it, Hazel thought.

"Well you look smashing...new jacket?"

"Logan's in the harbor, on sale." Hazel really did love the jacket though it hadn't been worn as planned. She had found herself hating the idea of traveling without John, who during those hard-earned trips always managed to make the world seem less gray when it rained and more colorful than a Moroccan bizarre when the sun was out. "I bought it thinking I'd like to go abroad again."

"I'm wearing the earrings you brought back from France," Ellis said pulling her hair back.

"That's where I picked up the little case with the snakeskin trim, the one John called my doctor's bag."

"Which I have coveted for years. If you ever get tired of it, you know what to do."

"You've been coveting things since you were a child, especially those cheap trinkets I picked up at the El Rastro in Madrid," Hazel said. "Maybe you should wear one of the bracelets as something old on your wedding day."

"And maybe your pearls for something borrowed?"

Hazel laughed in the way that John called a snort, but she couldn't help herself. "What's on the menu?" Hazel would not spoil her surprise. She'd taken Mother Mowry's pearls to the local jeweler to have the clasp repaired and while she was there, she'd bought Ellis's birthstone in the perfect size to be made into a pendant that would then attach to the pearls by an enhancer clip. The aquamarine stone couldn't have been more perfect if Hazel had designed the bridesmaids dresses herself.

"Does that mean I can't wear the pearls?"

"It means maybe I had something else in mind. Don't be so nosy. Now, what sounds good?"

"They're finally all set up: elegant white tablecloth, pretty china laid out with gleaming silverware and tiered stands heaped with two kinds of muffins and apple turnovers. And they have maple sausages."

Hazel couldn't say that her appetite had faded when the dance ended so she signaled the waitress for coffee, saying to Ellis, "I can't decide just yet."

"I'm thinking a couple of poached eggs with sausages." The minute that word left her mouth, Ellis knew how little willpower she had, even with a fitting coming up. Then she pulled the wedding buffet printouts from her tote. "You're going to need something substantial too. Take a look at the itemized list and price tag."

"I'm not here to quibble. You're my only granddaughter and John would have wanted us to do this up right. Besides, after the local charities, who can I spend it on?"

"I guess you're right; it should be me."

"Now you're talking."

"Do you miss him terribly?"

"Yes, I do. We had a good marriage, like I know you'll have." Hazel sensed the gravity of her response since Ellis would know nothing of those earliest years. "Not many young couples lived together when we got engaged, so it was hard to know what to expect other than looking to our parents and older friends and the way they handled married life." She waited for the waitress to fill her cup and walk away. "But we gals learned pretty quick that silly little arguments over dirty dishes or hair in the sink or who ate the last of the ice cream, were nothing more than a smoke screen for the bigger issues, and those were a lot harder to diagnose." Hazel said nothing of the hours left alone while John would be at one or another of the more popular watering holes hoping to catch the ear of a perspective client, perhaps a couple passing through or just one of the locals who had a need to change the scale of his house, only to come home tired and silent. Or the unexpected flare-ups—she hadn't lived in a house with a man since her teens, and with Midge in charge, adult tantrums wouldn't have been tolerated anyway. "I'm sure your grandfather would have shared his list of issues if you'd asked."

"I'm not so sure," Ellis said. "He always seemed to share the funny stories, like when you fell out of the dinghy while it was tied to the dock."

"He would tell you that one, but he had his complaints too." Hazel always believed the silences were the worst. It had taken many years for her to let those be, to consider them a part of his creative process, to not take it personally and especially not take her daughter and walk out once Janet was of school age. "But you're starting out differently."

"You're different here," Ellis said.

"That's because you've only known me as Gran, not the young woman with my own set of dreams. I thought after college, I might try my hand at writing or maybe with John's encouragement, possibly go into business with one of my classmates or even going back and getting my Masters. I just didn't think I was cut out for staying home full time."

"You always seemed so happy and content."

"We made it work, and I believe you will too no matter what you choose to do. Don't think I haven't noticed how you're stewing about this, but Artie is a fine young man."

"I called him earlier. Things have been going so fast that I woke up with the oddest thought that I'm making another mistake," Ellis said. "I just needed to hear his voice."

Hazel cringed; as with disappointments, she'd had to make friends with many of her own mistakes. "It's perfectly natural, and what happened with that terrible man is all in the past."

"I know, but Mom said you and Gramps had a short breakup before your wedding. I don't want that to happen either."

"You'll be fine." Hazel felt a tightening in her chest—a guilty conscience no less. Janet meant no harm, but she suffered from a malady—verbal diarrhea—a seemingly incurable state that had become more prominent in recent months, and caused new rifts to open, which often left Hazel flummoxed by it all. She stuffed down her nanosecond of remorse before saying, "Don't you go worrying about that; your mother doesn't always know what she's talking about."

"Dad's going to hate all this pomp." Ellis was named for her paternal great-grandmother and that ancestral tree had been borne from English stock going so far back that the males had titles. Barons and Earls graced the family crests, the likes of which she'd never seen before her research. The thatched-roof villages were small and the titled men ruled over farmstock and not very grand plots of land. But it was Hazel's maternal side that Ellis still struggled with, and so far, she'd only been able to trace as far back as the Isle of Wight, though she wasn't giving up. Through hours of secretive research, she'd uncovered possible links to families whose surnames were still listed in the Boothbay Peninsula phone books because so many from those British Isles had somehow made their way to Maine: fishmongers, sailmakers, artists and even one responsible for a long-standing eatery noted for their seasonal hot dogs and fried clams.

"Just give him time; I know he wanted you to be married out on the lawn under a big white tent at the Mowry house, but this is so much nicer."

"It's funny how we all still call it that."

"Not really. John made it his business to record many homes on the coastline that maintained their original name. He was quite the historian and loved those big old houses with their widow's walk along the tops and liked to say the houses were a lot like boats changing hands and how often the seamen wouldn't change the name in case it brought bad luck. But then, John could weave a good tale out of old rope."

"I heard there was a petition to change the name of the street back to Fisher's Hill."

"Better make sure you get a copy to your brother." Jake was next in line and had every intention of keeping everything about the house as it had always been. And unlike Linden, Jake was adept at woodworking. But that was before he'd been shipped off to some dusty outpost in the Middle East.

"Mom's beside herself, and Dad wanted to call the Pentagon to have Jake sent back in time for the wedding."

"Sounds like Linden, but this is one of the hardest things to wait out, and there's nothing to be done but wait."

"Speaking of waiting, what's really going on with these little trips to the ballroom?"

"Nostalgia more than anything and thinking about John and the way we were in those photos. And remembering Sloane and all the other friends I've lost. It's just a lot to process and unavoidable now that I'm here.

"And, if you promise not to laugh, I wanted to see if I could remember the time when I first learned about dancing a tango." Hazel knew she'd burst if she didn't mention the dance out loud at least once even if it meant weaving a tale or two of her own to protect her late husband's memory.

"What!"

"That's right, your old Gran had a tango lesson right in that very ballroom, the same place you and your friends will be dancing whatever it is you call it these days."

"Forget about us. Tell me about you."

"Let's have some breakfast first and talk about your reception, and then we can discuss my dancing."

~

"You were right about one thing," Hazel said. "Those apple thingies were fantastic!"

"Tarts, Gran."

"*Whatever.*"

"Are you mocking me?"

"Heavens, no. It's not like I haven't heard you say that a thousand times since you were a teenager."

"Help me somebody," Ellis implored the air above. "My Gran's losing it."

"Oh, all right, but I need to know if you really want that ordinary buffet when you can have those magnificent plated dinners?"

"Have you added up what the cost would be for seventy-four guests?"

"What happened to the seventy-fifth?"

"It was actually seventy-six, until we found out that Jake can't take leave. Maybe you could call the Pentagon."

"Now you're just being cheeky, but believe me, I would if I could."

"Artie's brother-in-law can't come either, but to be perfectly honest, he's such a snob, he won't be missed."

"I should really ask Millie, but then I don't want to be a third wheel, and you can't very well leave Fred off the invitation."

"Gramps and Fred used to play golf together, right?"

"He was part of their Saturday foursome, and the last to see John before he died. That's how Millie and I got to be such good friends these last ten years, what you'd call golfing widows."

"I really like Millie. Maybe June could be your plus one and you can all sit together."

"I think she's going to be away all of August." As far as Hazel could tell, they were only third or fourth cousins, but June had saved her from taking in a movie alone or when she didn't feel like cooking for one, going to a restaurant together. Any number of things for which she had never wanted to rely on her married friends. If only she hadn't let John rely on her quite so much, she thought tuning back in to Ellis, suddenly filled with another kind of joy. Ellis would be marrying someone who would value her as an equal partner. No one could ask for more.

"Do you think the odd number is bad luck or is it simply that you'd prefer an escort?" Ellis said. "Maybe you could ask that nice man at the library I've seen you flirting with."

"I don't flirt, and yes, it would be nice to have someone my age to visit with while all the young people are dancing."

"It's your money, you don't need my blessing."

"I know that."

"But do you know that their four-course plated dinners would mean nearly six thousand dollars! Are you sure you want to be that extravagant?"

"Hazel's eyes flew open and her hands went to her chest. "I'm prepared to sell my jewels if necessary!"

"Okay then, go ahead and spend pots of money on me, your granddaughter extraordinaire."

"Yes, I will, because I'm biased and so was John, so let's make him proud, shall we? And before you get all teary-eyed, think of it as giving your mother something really big to talk about afterward."

Ellis rolled her eyes. "You're incorrigible!"

"Okay, start making notes," Hazel said. "Seventy-five Ocean Grand dinners, and instead of my asking her as my plus one, make sure you put her full name on my cousin's invitation—June Patten Webster; she'll like that. She probably can't come, and I don't want you to take that personally, but it is the right gesture." Hazel understood how their relationship was a source of pride in their shared Maine histories and how her ancestors merged eons ago with June's lineage on the Tibbett side, and how seldom June had a chance to share the small details, especially since so many harbor folks had their own recorded histories to untangle. Unbeknownst to Hazel until quite recently, June had discovered a homestead near Wiscasset in a spot once known as *Jeremysquam Island.*

"Did you know that some of my ancestors are buried on Westport Island?"

"I thought we were talking about food?" Ellis squirmed; had Gran caught on to her surprise after all? Before the new wedding date, Ellis's research had mired her in the realm of genealogy and DNA and like her grandfather's historical interests, she'd found total fascination in the notion of putting flesh on the bones of those who'd made the long ocean voyages. Many of those travelers had sadly been stripped of titles and sometimes dignity in the wake of new hierarchies and declarations and even war. It would take a while before she could predict the accuracy of her discoveries or even how much it would matter in the scheme of building a tree that would stay within the family. But it had become a much heftier project than she'd ever imagined. And right now, she could hardly believe it would ever be finished.

"We are," Hazel said leaning in. "Just curious, that's all."

"Is this sorbet necessary? It seems out of place in the middle of the menu choices."

"In my day, it was called an intermezzo, a palate cleanser," Hazel said.

"Sounds like mouthwash."

"Now who's being incorrigible?"

"Sorry, but I couldn't pass that up."

"What about the bar? Should we do a champagne toast and have a cash bar? If we're going to cut back on anything, that's where I'd suggest."

"Most of Artie's friends like the craft beers and there are plenty to choose from. And my friends like all different types of wines and cocktails, so a cash bar would eliminate us trying to figure out how to make everybody happy. But, from what I've been reading, doing that can seem a little tacky...inviting guests who have spent on travel and gifts and then make them pay for their own drinks."

"Maybe we could just provide beer and wine and leave it at that."

"If that's all right with you, then yes, let's do that," Ellis said. "I'll ask him which beer he'd prefer, and you and I can choose from the Colony's house wines. Agreed?"

"Agreed."

"While we're here, Gran, there is something I haven't even told Mom; it's about Artie's mother."

"It was a while back, but she seemed perfectly lovely to me."

"She's also perfectly meddling, and I know anything I say right now is going to sound so petty, but she's bugging the hell out of me."

"And here I thought it would be Janet causing tension. What's up with Marilyn Granger?"

"No offense, but for one thing, she's worse than you about ancestors. Full of southern piety about their Virginia relatives, and I didn't have the heart to point out that our two families were probably duking it out during the Civil War, and we all know who won that battle."

Hazel smiled. Linden would love getting into it with Artie's mother. But he never bragged about his family especially the old guard who'd done Maine proud. "A bit of prima donna?"

"Worse, she has this thing about divorce…none in her family going back generations, yadda, yadda, yadda. And

69

since I'm divorced, well you can imagine how it makes me feel. I certainly don't intend to have another one, but it's not like I have a crystal ball. We'll do the best we can, I suppose, like everyone does."

"Piety speaks and not always kindly," Hazel said. "It has always galled me that some people act as if divorce was contagious, like some sort of self-inflicted disease, and it's really none of their darn business."

"Artie doesn't quite get it, Gran, and I just want her to go away, which of course is both impossible and childish," Ellis said. "And Mom's going to blow a gasket when she finds out."

"She does love that boy, but I don't know what I can do. My experience with the Mowry's made everything easy when John and I got married, and cheaper not only because it was a smallish wedding, but he swallowed his pride and allowed them to foot the bill."

"Was there dancing?"

"You aren't going to let that go, are you?"

"Marilyn, shmarilyn, this has to be more fun. But let me go to the Ladies Room first so I can give you my full attention," Ellis said getting up from the table.

Hazel was selfishly happy she didn't have to wade through the mother-in-law situation, at least not this very moment, but how much more about the topic of dancing could she afford to say, she wondered as her eyes followed

Ellis toward the public restrooms? There were no guidebooks to consult, and how was she supposed to confess a story that hadn't had a happy ending in the traditional sense. And, seemed like some poorly written novel in which the protagonist hadn't a clue how to navigate the moments of her life. She sat up straight. *This was her story.*

"You look so pensive," Ellis said, sitting back down.

"I think it's something that comes with age, at least June has it down pat and she's as old as me."

"Does she know about your tango?"

"You're not to say anything to anyone!"

"Maybe just Artie," Ellis smirked.

"You're impossible, but here goes. It was a long time ago..."

"And there was a princess..."

"Don't be fresh."

"Sorry, go on... please."

"It's those darn photos. I hadn't looked at the album in years until your mother began going on and on about it. It was one of her childhood *dream* books, and she'd pretend she was the bride and of course she was far too young to even imagine a groom, but she'd stand in front of the mirror in my shoes and wearing some piece of material over her head and pretend it was a veil."

"Sounds adorable."

"She was, but I digress," Hazel said. "Almost as soon as you and I walked through those doors and checked in, it was like I'd never left. So much has stayed the same as it was when those old photographs were taken; the room décor, the layout, and it's hard to know whether its time altering my perspective or just faulty memories, or a little of both. Sounds silly, right?"

"More like intriguing."

"To try to put a little of it into some kind of context, your grandfather had somehow screwed up the courage to propose to me the night of Sloane's wedding. Who knows, maybe it was the booze or all that dancing that spurred him on. But, in truth, he also didn't think I'd say yes."

"Why not, you'd been going out long enough, hadn't you?"

"I was naïve once too, Ellis, and we'd known each other for what seemed like forever and I guess I wondered if that was enough because we'd also come from vastly different households. Don't ask me what I expected, but in the heat of the moment, he took me to my room, kissed me with abandon the likes of which I'd never experienced, and left, just like that."

"OMG!"

"Indeed! Well, that kept me awake and wondering, and *skulking* if I'm being really honest. I wandered around the hotel in a state of confusion—out by the pool, back through the great room and then down the long corridor where I *happened* on the wedding photographer playing music in the ballroom."

"*He* was your dance partner?"

"Sort of," Hazel said readjusting her position—hard seats were a bane to thin bones. "I started having these flashbacks earlier before you walked in there, and I could see myself standing back from the doorway where he couldn't see me and just listening to this strange sounding music." Hazel wouldn't be able to tell her how she'd remembered the name of the piece he'd been playing or the way it had moved her almost to tears, which would be giving away far too much.

"Was he as good looking as Gramps?"

Her ideals had changed just as she had, but she chose to believe her memory. "Different or foreign looking we probably would have said; don't forget it was Maine in 1963. *And he was so sure of himself that she'd wanted to drown in those eyes.* "My recollection is that he was working these weddings as a way to save money for his own studio, and when I was sitting back there this morning, I also remembered thinking, how wonderful, I could show John, and we'd show the Kaplans and we'd all go dancing together."

"And did you?"

Hazel preferred the lie. "Hardly...I never really learned."

"*Did* he open a studio?"

She thought of the times when her spirit seemed so low, she would have given anything to be held that way, to feel desired again, but those days had passed along with her youth, or at least that's what she'd preferred to believe. "I never really tried to find out, but thinking about it today, I wish I had. Again, this is another one of those little things that have been coming back in fits and starts—like what he'd said about giving private lessons in a loft in Portland. I think it was owned by a Russian who I believe now would probably have danced with a ballet company before coming to America."

"Like a Baryshnikov movie."

"Maybe, but it was a world beyond my imagination, exotic sounding and thrilling. I didn't even have a passport back then."

"There are dance studios all over Maine," Ellis said. "Do you think it's possible one of them might be his?"

Hazel hoped her face wouldn't betray her feelings; just the thought of Eduardo still being in semi-close proximity after so many years made her pulse quicken. "I honestly wouldn't know, but even as a clumsy novice, I knew he was good, and it was obvious the tango was his specialty." *Among other things.* Hazel sensed a band of red spots dotting their way across her forehead. She certainly couldn't tell Ellis how overwhelmed the attention had made her feel, or that she'd had a brief affair shortly after her grandfather proposed. "But that's all I'm giving you."

"Oh, come on, you can't stop now."

"I can too." What Hazel refused to say was that John had all but abandoned her when she needed him most, that she'd kept her virginity intact until the right moment, and that the proposal had been a giant leap in their relationship. Or that she'd already surmised and not happily, that his work might just take precedence over their marriage, and that like so many young women then—and maybe even now—she thought love would make it all better.

She wouldn't admit how she had tried to ignore the fact that to move up the ranks as an architect in a region where there wasn't much room in which to move, meant sacrificing personal time. There were all-night charrettes and working through weekends and holidays, and she still hadn't been sure of where she'd fit in.

And that with a broad smile and a huge apology he'd left her at the hotel to mull her fate while he went off to prepare for another all-nighter that would have him ready for a Monday morning client meeting, his future happily plotted out.

And she certainly couldn't spoil the day by saying she'd never forgotten the image of his 1957 Thunderbird — the car he'd so lovingly restored — a slash of bronze racing away from the Colony's parking lot, and how bereft his happiness had made her feel. *Vulnerable enough to be swept off her feet by a handsome stranger named Eduardo.* "I never meant to rehash all this; it's your weekend. But so much of what happened after Sloane's magnificent wedding, so many plans she'd made and shared while we were getting ready up there in those second-floor rooms…they're all squashed together up here," Hazel said tapping her skull. "Even words I'd written to her when I found out she was in such bad shape. It was like she'd been riding on my shoulder all the way from Boothbay Harbor, letting me know I had to find a way to let go."

"I'm glad to listen if you need me to."

"Believe it or not, your Marilyn reminds me a little of Sloane's mother. But the difference is that instead of being overprotective of her daughter, she was all about the new son-in-law."

"Please, she's not *my* Marilyn."

"Just an expression, dear, but Sloane's mom always reminded me of some Victorian woman who had a fainting couch in her parlor for when things became too difficult to manage. They were well off financially after Sloane's father died, at least compared to what we'd been used to, and everything had to be just right: Sloane's clothes, her hair, men she went out with, and then when it turned out the only thing her future son-in-law had going for him were his looks, old Ethyl took to her bed." Hazel could never tell Ellis about the rest—the pain Sloane disguised with laughter, or the night terrors when they had sleepovers. Hazel had promised not to tell a soul, not even Midge, who might have taken matters into her own hands, but Hazel had kept her word.

"God forbid this is what I'm dealing with," Ellis said.

"We'll get you a fainting couch as a wedding present and you can beat her to the punch," Hazel said. "But all kidding aside, this hotel was right out of a fairy tale and there again, Ethyl could have chosen one of the perfectly fine hotels in the harbor that could have easily accommodated the reception, but she wanted grand everything, and I think that had a lot to do with impressing Mike, though for the love of me, I can't think why.

"And don't get me wrong, all in all, we were a happy foursome for quite a long while, even without the dancing. Then things changed, and that's all very hard to dissect here in one go." Drinking the rest of her coffee, she plunked down her empty cup and said, "Now, what do we have planned for today? I'd like to walk off breakfast if we have enough time."

"Perfect. You can help me choose locations. Like Sloane, I want to have the candid shots of all of us fixing our hair and makeup in the rooms upstairs, which must be some kind of custom because Lara also suggested that. I loved the idea of having pictures of them all helping me with my gown and that tiresome veil."

"Do you need it?"

"Mom insisted, and I don't want to disappoint her."

"Then don't; the veil is one of those symbols and other than flowers in your hair, I don't know how else to complete the look. Besides, it'll look good for the more formal photos. And then there'll be the toasts and after that, you'll be able to ditch the veil for the rest of the festivities."

"I just don't want anything to seem too staged. That photographer, Peter Hamilton, gave me a couple of good suggestions."

"He must have been the man I saw when I first came downstairs, before you found me. Seemed intriguing in an odd sort of way, but then I really didn't pay much attention."

"He was a tad egotistical, but nice. I checked him out online, and I guess he has a reason for that ego because his work is fabulous! I told him why the water views meant so much to me, and he said there was a clearing here on the back lawn that might be promising."

"Promising it is then," said Hazel. "I'll just go get my coat and then I'll be ready. And then later let's go shopping and I'll treat you to dinner in town." Hazel relaxed a little. Ellis was going through the typical pre-wedding emotions, perhaps more so because of Marilyn Granger, but nothing any Beane woman couldn't handle. Had she lived, Midge would have given one of her standard pep talks, something along the lines of 'tell her where to stuff it', and Ellis for all her good manners, did have a knack for similar outbursts. But there had to be another way to combat her future mother-in-law. Hazel might have spent hours wending her way through their gene pool, but she'd exhausted her ability to continue, so she simply gave Ellis an enigmatic smile and went back up to her room—this time with an unfiltered image of Eduardo to accompany her. They'd also walked the grounds, searching for nothing, while finding the extraordinary. They'd ended up huddled together on the beach in the pre-dawn hours as he continued to teach her about the music he'd been playing: *Verano Porteno* by Astor Piazzola. Eduardo couldn't have known that even when stilled, the music would stay with her for a lifetime. He elicited promises she believed at the time she'd never keep. Then, as if it was the most natural thing in the world, he too left her alone to mull her fate.

Chapter 8

Hazel's room at the end of the hall had been put back together; no offending sheets holding onto bad dreams, nothing to indicate the existence of a difficult period of time, not even a hint of her distress. Peeking into the adjoining room, which was also neat and tidy, a sudden sense of shame came over her; she'd taken so much time away from Ellis's day because of a long-lost dream. For both their sakes, it was now time to pay attention to the present. And for starters, this meant dabbing on fresh lipstick and bypassing the mirror, which had so honestly pointed out that she was far from perfect, but definitely good enough! Grabbing the raincoat that she'd traveled in, Hazel rushed back out without paying attention to the sound of the door as it slammed behind her.

Once outside, she threw her arms up in salutation—piercing spring sunshine without wind was one of the best cures after a long Maine winter. *Maybe that young man was able to capture something worthwhile after all,* she thought as her eyes searched for Ellis. The good weather had also brought out the missing guests and from Hazel's perspective near the pool, the width and breadth of the Colony all but filled the sky. The hotel's heritage had been transformed over a century of remakes, including a fire that had destroyed the original building. And then, like a phoenix risen from the ashes of history, it fought for its place among the premier hotels of Maine. Her own transformation hadn't been quite as dramatic, but it sure had shaken things up. *Memories were like laundry,* she thought, and some of them didn't have to be aired on the line for all to see. But she couldn't do a thing about accidentally eavesdropping on the couples by the pool: "The food here is supposed to be top-notch." "We should have brought the dog." "Why did I let you talk me out of bringing my bathing suit." "Do you have Wi-Fi 'cause we couldn't get reception." Hazel nodded and smiled at that particular guest who was huddled in a sweater as she reclined on a deck chair, but she felt it better not to add her two cents. The hotel was known to be particularly dog friendly and the food was superb or she wouldn't be paying a small fortune for the reception. But as she scanned the grounds, Hazel also thought of the burden of an opinionated mother-in-law and silently implored the gods to go easy on her granddaughter; she'd been through enough. But she also thought of John and how things might have played out had he lived. Suddenly, she heard her name and turned in a small circle until she saw Ellis, whose head appeared like a golden bonnet on the knoll. "Coming," Hazel called out. Ellis, in a rather curious stance, was framing a scene without her camera, but using her fingers as a viewfinder.

"I should have guessed you'd be out here staring at the water," Hazel said as she moved in closer.

"Just having a little fun with an idea," Ellis replied. "But what I really wanted you to see is on the far side of the hotel."

Linking arms, Ellis took the lead, guiding Hazel over uneven ground until it leveled out to a cushiony, green lawn. On this side, the breeziness turned into a gentle kiss of fragrant air. The waves below, furrowed and soft. "This is it, Gran."

It truly was a window on the Atlantic. The wide sunlit vista was framed by well-pruned bushes and reached by a stone path ending at a circular stone landing. "Perfect," Hazel said. "Either for the ceremony or the after-photos, whichever you prefer."

"I love it!" Ellis said.

A lone schooner sliced through deep water, its rigging taut and its bow proud, a classic postcard from Maine. "Being with John made me realize I had a true affinity for the sea, and none of that comes from my kin. Once they'd crossed from England to Massachusetts and the colonies split, they mostly ended up in Somerset County, homesteading places like the one I showed you."

"There was one window that hadn't been totally boarded up; talk about a humble existence."

"That it was, but I just had to go back one more time before the place fell into more ruin, and one of the old neighbors had called me to let me know those magnificent giant chestnut trees were about to be cut down. They'd been my favorite and there wasn't anything I could do about it. Plus, I wanted you to see the Moscow and Bingham cemeteries in case you ever wanted to know where a few of the family ghosts are buried."

"I wouldn't have missed it for the world."

"Well, ghosts or no, they've been long gone, and we're here in the right spot for a seaside wedding. And, thankfully, your bridesmaids will be wearing dresses that can handle the wind if it kicks up. It was so embarrassing to have to keep holding our skirts down."

"That's why we chose a longer and straighter style, but there are no guarantees the weather will cooperate, and that's why they pay Lara the big bucks," Ellis said. "She also happens to live on the coast, and after a few wedding disasters caused by the unexpected, she's mapped all this stuff out for her brides—therefore, we have an alternative spot and there's a shortcut on the way to her office."

"What are we waiting for, then," Hazel said. "Spring means renewal, sweetie, and this is going to be the grandest wedding ever!"

"Oh, Gran," Ellis said. "What would I ever do without you?"

"Best we keep walking before I get all weepy." This entire excursion was about renewal, Hazel mused, and they'd both be the better for it.

"This is what I was talking about." Ellis had stopped in front of a small portico just beyond Lara's office. "I kind of like this, don't you?"

"It'd be okay as long as the sun cooperates. You need the proper backlighting to make a dramatic silhouette. But I'd rather this than that dark paneled room you showed me first," Hazel said. "Does Artie get an opinion or maybe even your mom and dad merit a vote, unless you're determined to figure all this out on your own."

"Remind you of anyone," Ellis said. "I've been channeling Gramps, trying to view everything from his perspective, and not doing a bang-up job of it."

"You are doing just fine. That phone of yours can do the rest. Take the pictures and post them or send them through cyberspace or however you do with them, and when you get their replies, you can make your final choice. And, you do still have time to change your mind about the where, just not the when."

"I'll do that next, but it'll be hard to photograph the portico without a stand-in for the full effect."

"We can take another swing-through before dinner and if the light's right, you can use me as your stand-in." Hazel said. "And by the way, I hope they are paying her the big bucks; she's a real treasure." They hadn't used wedding planners in Hazel's day, just copied and made better than the brides before them, and of course there were always magazines featuring glamorous women to try and emulate.

"We hit it off right from the start," Ellis said. "But it was genius what she did with the magnetic board for the seating chart."

"Reminded me of Monopoly without the fake money," Hazel said.

"If so, then Artie would toss the 'sweetheart' table into jail and throw away the key. He's not going to like being isolated off to one side of the wedding party like that," Ellis said. "And then, its where we're going to seat the parents—Marilyn and Mom might clash and Dad is such a pussycat. The plan is all there for us to work out, but I'm just not prepared, am I?"

"It'll all come together when you get home and you and Artie have a chance to hash it all out. And your mom and dad are not novices to polite society, you know, it's not like they have anything to prove."

"I know, Gran, and I'm being a big baby. My guess is

it's more about wanting Marilyn to be as happy for us as my family is."

"You can pick your friends, dear, but not your relatives, so buck up and make your plans strictly for you and your groom, not for the rest of us."

"I really love you."

"I know honey…now what's next?"

"Like Lara said, tomorrow's the cake tastings, so you and I have the rest of the day to ourselves.

"What was the name of the one that looked like a waterfall?"

"Ombre, like our dresses, one shade flowing into the next."

"I guess as long as it tastes good, I shouldn't care that I never heard the name before."

"You and your sweet tooth," Ellis said.

"Does Artie have a choice?"

"The only way to make us both happy no matter the design, was to make sure the cake has both chocolate layers and white, not yellow cake because they don't taste the same. Mrs. Anthony makes white cakes like that for special occasions and she uses almonds for the filling, but since it's Artie's favorite, we're substituting with pistachio cream."

"And we have to wait till tomorrow to taste it?"

"Have a big dessert tonight to tide you over, and how come you never gain weight?"

"It's a Beane thing, you'll see."

"Are you looking for anything in particular in town?" asked Ellis.

"Besides a pair of beige flats, I need to buy gifts for two upcoming birthdays, and I promised Millie I'd look out for a sushi serving platter and bowl set. We've decided to try our hand at making them, and she has the kit."

"Aren't you two ambitious!"

"Use it or lose it, or so they say."

"I've always wondered who *they* were, but it sounds like fun. Not the type of dishes on our registry, which was one of the only things I didn't have to change. There's nothing listed remotely connected to raw seafood—Artie likes fried everything."

"Give it time, dear, you'll see how he'll adapt."

"Don't you have a handbook or something you can loan me; you seem to have done a lot of adapting."

"Maybe we'll write one together one day." Hazel thought of all the advice she'd been given and the things she'd ignored. No one ever really had the answers, but it didn't hurt to try. "Now let's get going."

"Do you have to change again?"

"Now that's just plain mean."

"Just keeping you on your toes."

"Speaking of, I'd better change my shoes."

"See!"

"You know what they say about the golden egg?"

"Oops, I'll shut up."

"That's better; now go along and I'll meet you at the car."

Chapter 9

By late afternoon, Dock Square was abuzz with traffic, and other than different makes and models of cars and an obvious difference in hair styles, the busy scene was very much as Hazel recalled. Kennebunkport wasn't as fussed up as some of the other coastal towns hit with the tourist boom, but there was the same obvious pride in its appearance: boldly decorated window boxes and hanging pots; swept-clean cobbled walks and gleaming storefront windows; notable restaurants, and for Hazel, a chance later on to get a glimpse of the presidential compound on Walker's Point.

Within minutes of parking the car, Hazel and Ellis were surrounded by shoppers who like them, seemed to be trying to decide what to do first, and accidentally found themselves in step behind a young family whose small boy was pointing and jumping and pulling them toward a menu board bigger than his sturdy little body. It was the *Spirit of Massachusetts,* all restored and turned into a unique floating restaurant. "Obviously, this wasn't here in the '60s—you can't miss something this big pushed up to the street," Hazel said. "John would have gotten such a kick out of this."

"I like it here."

"We all did too, but then we never would have been here in the first place if it hadn't been for Sloane's cousin," Hazel said. "We'd never thought about finding a *destination* venue like you girls do now, and besides, neither of us had a ring on our finger at the time."

"It's been that way in Maine for years, and of course, that's why the computer makes it so easy to find the right one."

"We were only here to shop and poke around and drink the eighty-cent martinis her cousin had raved about, though looking back, I can't see why she'd have thought they tasted different from drinks served in the harbor. Anyway, we thought maybe we'd do a little sightseeing if we had time."

"Eighty cent drinks, what planet was this?"

"The same planet that served preset dinners for under five-dollars!"

"Oh, if only," Ellis said. "Our bar tab alone will be enough to feed a small country!"

"Nonsense," Hazel said. "But I'm sure we'd had too much to drink, and had to walk it off which is how we ended up in the hotel parking lot. If my memory's right, we'd gone inside to use the restroom and then ended up wandering through like a couple of country bumpkins, gaping at everything until by the time we walked into the ballroom, and I swear Sloane said this—'When I get married, it's going to be in this very ballroom'."

"Talk about fate," Ellis said.

"The real stroke of fate was meeting Mike not long after she'd said it."

"I guess then it's watch what you wish for."

"I suppose, but she was besotted in those early months, as people in love are supposed to be."

"You and your novels."

"It's that first blush of romance, and yes, it does sound like a work of fiction, but then maybe love should be able to stay that way for a while, before life takes over and makes everything hard."

"I'll settle for over the moon if that's okay; besotted is probably why I married the angry penis."

"I think we can stow that away, don't you?" Hazel said. "Besides, it's time to shop."

"My bad; how about I just duck into that leather store across the street, and we'll pretend I'm a grownup."

"You're quite grown up; you just sounded a lot like your great-grandmother Midge," Hazel said. "But then again, if that stuff had happened to me, I'd probably do the same. Now, I'm starting on this side of the street and will meet you in front of the Hurricane Restaurant, say in forty-five minutes?"

"Perfect." Ellis headed for the crosswalk.

Hazel watched her go thinking of the times Ellis really did sound like Midge—outspoken and given to language maybe more suited to mixing it up with the men she'd been exposed to since working in the harbor. And then Hazel thought of all the words she had suppressed when their release might have made her feel better. She'd held so much in over the years, been so perfectly turned out and proper, the wife of an ambitious man, and all that had gotten her was a peptic ulcer. *And now,* she thought, will the same stomach pain return or could she soothe it away with new beginnings? Maybe she just couldn't win, but she could shop, and she just happened to be standing right in front of the pottery store.

Chapter 10

Inside and out, the iconic restaurant with the ominous sounding name was the perfect place to end their shopping experience. There were panoramic views of the Kennebunk River on what had turned out to be a balmy afternoon, and Hazel and Ellis and their multiple shopping bags were seated near a bank of windows overlooking the water.

"This place wasn't here either," Hazel said. "But their menu looks fabulous." She had checked at the hotel and been given good reviews and a menu to look at ahead of time. And so far, she wasn't disappointed with anything. The building was on pilings, which gave the diner the effect of floating on the water, and at this hour, the breeze was barely an afterthought, and not enough to disturb a thick shadow cast beneath the hull of a white dory attached by a painter to an orange mooring ball.

Hazel beamed and pointed to a duck and a raft of ducklings skittering toward shore and a cluster of fallen branches. "Love the wildlife."

Ellis followed Hazel's gaze. "This is exactly the kind of place Mom would love. Do you think there's any chance they'd stay over an extra night?"

"I wouldn't bank on it. Linden doesn't like being away from the store for too long during the season, but it's worth suggesting."

Exuberance was in the air, and if she listened carefully, Hazel could make out the zeal of a seasoned shopper and the exhausted voice from a delighted sightseer as they mingled with the anticipation of a menu that boasted some of the finest dishes on the Coast of Maine, though Hazel knew there were a few back in Boothbay Harbor who would give them a run for their money. But by the time she smelled the aromatic herb wafting off the breadbasket, she felt like she was in an alternate universe. Food was one of the main reasons she'd always loved traveling, and meeting new people, and suddenly she was back in Italy. "Rosemary," she said to the young man dressed in black like all the waitstaff. She'd always believed a uniform look made dining out feel more important. "Did you know it's known as the herb of love?"

Putting a small saucer of olive oil next to the bread, he said, "Your waitress will be with you shortly."

Hazel waited until he was a few feet away, and said, "I made him blush."

"He's hardly more than a boy in training." Ellis's eyes lingered as he stopped next to a nearby table, kneeling in front of one of the tots who seemed to be showing off a breadstick. She turned back to her grandmother. "Are you pleased with your necklace?"

"Not that I needed another piece of jewelry, but yes, I love it. You didn't do so bad yourself with that leather clutch, especially the color."

Ellis patted the turquoise pouch, clinking her engagement ring on the clasp. "I guess I'm in my blue period."

"I got everything I needed, especially since I didn't have to walk miles, and I can honestly say, I'm shopped out."

"This is a nice experience for me since I buy almost everything online these days."

"Where's the fun in that?"

"None, but it's easy, that's why it works."

Hazel didn't expect to broach the topic, but this was her cue. Ellis's eyes had been darting back and forth to the same table ever since they'd sat down. "Have you and Artie talked about kids?"

"What made you think of that now?"

"The way you've been glancing at those toddlers across the room. I must say, they're really well behaved for such little guys."

"Of course, we've talked about it." Ellis's tone had been sharper than she'd intended. No one but Jeanie and Artie knew about the miscarriage she'd had before leaving

Walter. "Sorry Gran, that didn't come out right—we just haven't figured out when. How about we drive over toward Walker's Point later on and see if there's any activity."

Hazel knew when to hold her tongue. "I think I read where the Bush's don't arrive till June, but it's been on my bucket list. Did you know that political strategy sessions were once held in the hotel conference center?"

"Now why would I know that?"

"By paying more attention to politics, for instance," Hazel said. "And I thought it was one of those fun factoids to remember since we're staying here."

"I pay attention, Gran. I vote, I recycle, I worry about climate change, but things seem such a mess that I mentally throw up my hands and forget about it because it's too depressing."

"All the more reason for you to get involved."

"Not now, Gran, please."

This was a topic about which she refused to hold her tongue. "At least follow the Letters to the Editor in the *Register* so you'll get a feel for your community again." Unlike her cousin, she no longer searched the obituaries; June would let her know if there was a service requiring Hazel's attendance. She preferred the Letters section of the local paper and the outrage and push-pull of the townsfolk over even the smallest details of the way their town was run. Lively discussions or outright anger carried on in print was a far cry from planning a funeral—a task made clear in her will after her last doctor's appointment and the addition of cholesterol medication. And reading obituaries offered no particular motivation to get up in the morning. "You're right, you'll find your way through the political maze soon enough. And this is not the time or place," she offered with less conviction than she would have preferred. Ellis was even prettier in the glow of the restaurant lighting, more than likely thinking of Artie, and here Hazel sat, all pinched around the mouth and ready to burst and wanting to add that apathy in politics would only make matters worse. But this was not the time to speak up. And because of her own involvement with the wedding, she was doing her best to navigate her way with this younger generation. "Someone told me the crab cakes here are terrific!" That was about all the brightness Hazel could offer in lieu of becoming a sourpuss.

"I think I'll have the same, and maybe we could split a Caesar salad. Looking at all that food earlier has taken away some of my usual appetite, and I suppose it's also time I paid attention to my pre-wedding waistline." Ellis had caught the eye of the waitress just a few feet away.

"We'll have that California Chardonnay to go with," Hazel said as soon as Ellis ordered. "And one check." Hazel watched as the waitress wrote in her little pad and left, and then she said, "You're a lot like me, sweetheart, you'll burn it off quickly."

"Poor Mom."

"I know, but then how can anyone resist those luscious pies she bakes?"

"I want her and Dad to feel like they're included in as much as possible even though we're taking the lead, so I thought we'd wrap up some cake to take home with us tomorrow, and I can drop it off after I leave you."

Once they'd ordered, Hazel settled in with a sense of irony about their little venture to Kennebunkport. Ellis's generous attitude was not unlike John's, who could be magnanimous to a fault. But he could also hoard his nickels, which had endeared him to Midge, the saver of small coins. John had bonded with Hazel's frugal roots. With her grandiose wedding, Sloane had thrown her father's legacy in his dead face. Hazel had felt security in her marriage. Sloane had lost more than her identity in hers. And Ellis's well-being would be front and center with a husband like Artie. Hazel's thoughts were beginning to unravel: the aftermath of that October wedding and her own subsequent rush to the altar, and now since she'd just thrown politics into the mix, *Camelot*. How had she not remembered a name not only synonymous with a zest for life, but with one of the most exciting and saddest times in American history—the months surrounding the candidacy and subsequent presidency of John Fitzgerald Kennedy. Or how it was in that highly charged atmosphere right there on Pear Street in Boothbay Harbor when the small presidential motorcade passed them by, that Sloane first met Mike. Hazel had watched them as if in a film, two beautiful people gravitating toward each other with such an obvious attraction that Hazel had imagined hearing the lyrics to *Strangers in the Night*. She'd later told John that her best friend had lost her heart that day. By then, Hazel had desired similar sparks in her relationship with him: steady, reliable, shy John. Of course, he was the devil's own handsome, Midge often said when describing him, and Hazel loved John's looks and had thankfully developed a deep love for the more mature version of the man she'd married. But only now, in the latter third of her life, with her heart shedding its long marital grip, would she admit to the fire and ice of Eduardo's nature and its effect on her in the all-too-brief period they'd spent together.

"You've gone off somewhere again."

"No, I'm paying attention, but I suddenly remembered that JFK was assassinated the month after Sloane's wedding."

"Holy…"

"Yes, it was a horrible time," Hazel said lowering her voice, hoping Ellis would take the cue.

"That was the movie, the one with Keven Costner that I was watching half the night last night. I'd seen it before, but that's all that I could find," Ellis whispered.

"With everything else we've been up to, I'd forgotten all about the time frame until just now," Hazel said. "But I don't want you to think I've forgotten about this nonsense with Marilyn. A bit of advice...if you're really worried about your relationship, now is the time to speak up, not after the wedding."

"I know, Gran, but she's still *his* mother. And as irritating as Mom can be, she's not the one suggesting we shouldn't have pets because she's allergic, among a lot of other non-essential things."

"Oh Ellis, that's ridiculous; you can't live your lives that way. Marilyn will just have to do what the rest of us do—take an antihistamine!"

"Let's face it, Gran, I'm venting all this nonsense because I'm afraid to rock the boat; Artie's a good man."

"If you don't mind my saying, you could try a little pillow talk with that good man of yours. That often solves a lot of domestic issues, and I speak from experience. Sometimes it was the only way I could reach your grandfather. People don't always talk about their feelings in the light of day. Then little things turn into bigger issues. And, while I don't mean to blather on about this stuff about Mike and Sloane, she let things slide along, not wanting to rock the boat either, but when she got sick, he was the one making the important decisions, not her," Hazel said.

"But that's different, Gran."

"Yes, illness is something else altogether, but a doormat is a doormat, and not something you'd ever want to be. And, if Artie's the man I think he is, he'll understand."

"I think I've got the picture."

"Good girl," Hazel said as she pulled a tissue from her bag. Ellis was, and hopefully would remain, untouched by the ugliness of a cruel disease. But all this talked only reminded Hazel of the way Sloane looked on one of the last days they'd spent together. She'd lost all her hair by then and on that day because it was just Hazel, Sloane had taken off the bright bandanna, one of the many she'd worn in honor of the hippie movement, along with her peace-symbol tee shirts. She had even hung onto the bellbottoms, thinking they'd one day come back into fashion. And for Hazel's sake, Sloane was going for the jokes instead of verbalizing what was taking place in her body. But Hazel saw a wariness in Sloane's eyes as if questioning her own ability to hold everything together, because she had been the strong one while Hazel was dying inside at the thought of what was coming. *She'd promised.* Sloane had elicited a promise from her on that long-ago March day as they sat in the well-appointed living room of the Kaplan house with a fire going, drinking tea and planning. The cancer had metastasized to her liver by then and while Mike refused to accept the medical verdict, Sloane had already contacted a hospice nurse for what she knew was inevitable. And Hazel was supposed to make sure Sloane's wishes were carried out. "Forgive me, sweetie, I can get a little carried away sometimes just thinking about what happened." Hazel felt the air deflating around her, and thought she saw a small shadow cross Ellis's face. Pity perhaps, or something else, it was hard to tell. Just then, the young waiter returned with the dessert menu. "Oh, look, they have Crème Brulee!"

"Sounds good. Should we split one of those too?" Ellis asked.

"Absolutely not!" Hazel's mood had quite naturally been shifting all day, but dessert was also good for the soul. She immediately piped up, "We'll have two large ones, please."

'You made him blush again, Gran."

"I have a knack."

Within moments, the boy had returned with what looked to be standard sized ramekins, and Ellis said, "This will do nicely."

"I know…your waistline," Hazel said digging in.

"Cheers," Ellis said clinking her spoon to Hazel's.

"Is there anything better than cracking through that

crust?"

"Maybe just eating a second one."

"Did I just inhale it?" Hazel said looking at the empty dish.

"Look who's talking," Ellis said licking her spoon. "Maybe we should take that drive before I lose my willpower."

"Speaking of driving, I am so sorry I sold your grandfather's old hardtop convertible. I imagine Artie would have treasured it."

"I never gave it a thought at the time, but it's too late now," Ellis said. "We'll just have to hang cans and a Just Married sign off the back of his truck."

"Don't be silly, we'll hire one of those limos for your departure photos, everything done up right, remember?"

"You really are too much," Ellis said. "Now let's get going before we lose the light."

Hazel stayed behind to pay the bill while Ellis got the car out of the lot. She left a substantial tip since she knew what it was like to wait tables and the hours spent on tired feet.

~

"This is a really pretty drive." Hazel hadn't been this far along Ocean Avenue before and wondered how many of the large homes were new.

"I had my mind made up about seeing this while I had the chance." Ellis pulled the car into a small cut-away, which she believed was not allowed when the President was in residence. They got out of the car and stood close to the large boulders and stared at the compound. "Wish I had a dime for all the Massachusetts plates I've seen today."

"Tis the season, and pretty soon tourists will be flocking in from everywhere to see what we have to offer. I once saw a license plate from Hawaii parked at Hannaford's in the harbor."

"Unfortunately, we can't really see much from here. Not even a nightlight twinkling from inside one of the rooms, unless there are blackout curtains so we can't see what's going on behind closed doors. Wonder what it'd be like to live in a place like that?"

"Expensive, but you can dream. Or you can enjoy that." Hazel pointed to the stars just breaking through. "And, they're free."

"Gramps always said, make a wish."

"That he did, and we always did. And so many of them came true," Hazel said. For all the memories that were invading her brain cells this weekend, she would forever be grateful to the man who'd given her some of the greatest ones. She wanted so much for Ellis to be able to say this in her later years, but there were no guarantees.

Sloane, the most deserving of brides had proven that.

"I think we're going to be okay, Gran."

"And I think I know what you wished," Hazel said getting back in the car.

CHAPTER 11

There's a place somewhere between sleep and waking where dreams are still in progress but not fully exposed to the light of day. Slowly opening her eyes, a vestige of those stars still glowed beneath Hazel's lids, lingering over the hilltops on their final trip to Italy. John died a year later. With all their good fortune, they couldn't ward off the unexpected no more than anyone could. Perhaps he'd had an omen, though, because he'd been hell-bent on that trip, needing to revisit the old villas with their rust-colored tiles, and study the way the light embellished the rough stucco finishes, which often changed colors with each passing hour. They'd romanticized the winding, chariot-sized roads too small for their rental car, eaten far too much, sampled all the wine they possibly could, and taken pleasure in the Italian way of living in the moment. And, so they had, which in the end turned out to be rather fortuitous. But, also in her dream was the gauzy yellow haze draped over lavender mountains, like looking at the mornings through a filtered lens.

She got out of bed and raised the multi-paned window as far as it would go, wishing there were old, patinaed shutters to fling open. But the smell was all wrong. Instead of the rich earthy fragrance of harvest time in the hills of

Italy, the scent was the clean, sharp smell for which seaside living was known. She closed the window and looked at the all-too-cheery profusion of unscented flowers that decorated the walls and sat back down on her bed.

There was a light tap at the adjoining door. Ellis peeked her head in, "I heard you moving around. Can I bring you some coffee?"

"That would be grand," Hazel said. Ellis was wearing a blue long-sleeved sweater and slim-leg jeans. "And don't you look nice this morning."

"Thanks, Gran, I'll be back in a jiff."

Hazel stared at the closing door. Thanks to John and whatever time he could carve out for them, teaching them about humanity on whatever level they'd been able to understand at the time, both grandchildren had turned into thoughtful, caring adults with a healthy sense of humor.

They had tried those same lessons with Janet in the earliest of years, but it was as if she'd come from another mold, some faraway place that left her always feeling a want of things she didn't have. Now, of course, it was far too late to hypothesize about any of that. Hazel could only give what was left of her maternal attributes, and today was probably not the day to dig too deep.

Without John, she'd put on her best face, volunteered wherever there was a need, and put one foot in front of the other like any good soldier marching toward the unknown. But being here with Ellis and sharing what was appropriate, felt to Hazel like a good kick in the pants for what had been ailing her.

There was a keen sense that she was ready to explore whatever had been so daunting; talents that had gone untended until they no longer counted and even a love that had been passed over. Was it too little too late, she wondered?

Putting on her bold-colored dressing gown to herald in a new day and this rather unique reasoning, she went to her overnight bag for the gift she had intended for Ellis. That was before she realized that Ellis and her friends were navigating the wedding details with the use of their smartphones, the likes of which Hazel had yet to decipher.

She held the notebook up to the light. The metallic gold cover shimmered and what looked like Chinese brush painting formed a tree with dark lines definitively scrolled by a fine hand. The cover opened from right to left like an actual book, and the lined pad inside was just right for her less-than-perfect handwriting. If handled like a diary, it could be a lovely reminder of their special time together, something Ellis might cherish after Hazel was gone. She found the hotel pen on the small writing desk, pulled out the accompanying chair, and thought about the way to frame a collection of missives that would begin with this weekend and end on her part with the August wedding. And then, if Ellis chose, she could add to it after the honeymoon.

They'd already accomplished a lot in a short time and there was still more to do before they arrived back home. But the last thing Hazel wanted was for her writings to turn into a mere outline of necessary tasks.

And yet, with the virgin pages open and ready for the first stroke of ink, she seemed unable to extract the myriad humorous and decorous decrees informed by years of experience and attendance at many other weddings and now meant to be jotted down for posterity. Instead, she found after only two pages, she'd written what could have been a sales pitch for hotel management.

And then when she tried to idealize the shades of blue that created the unique bond they would always share because of the Colony, it wasn't Ellis's wedding that propelled the pen, but thoughts of Sloane's. After that, Hazel had given up, put the notebook away and sat back down on the edge of her bed. Her wonderful plan had been hijacked by those terrible days in March of '84—and Mike Kaplan, and the forgiveness she still hadn't been able to roust from its secret place.

~

"Here we are," Ellis said pushing through the door with a tray. "Are you okay?"

"Of course, why?" Hazel offered with a breezy smile.

"I don't know; you had such a faraway look when I came in."

"What do they say in the movies—'fuhgettabout it'?"

"God, Gran, with your Maine-speak, *The Sopranos* would have been off the air before their second episode."

"I'll have you know I was much appreciated in stage performances during college."

"Gramps told me you only had two lines in *The Boy Friend*, and that can hardly be considered performances."

"Don't be cruel."

"Please tell me you weren't just referencing Elvis."

"I'll never tell. Now please, may I have my coffee?"

"Sorry. I'll pour. Or be Mother…isn't that what the Brits say when they share tea?"

"Listen to you."

"I slept better, but now I have new butterflies in my stomach about seeing our cake. I am such a sucker for those baking shows, even though I've had to make peace with the fact that I cannot bake worth a damn, not even from a box mix, and my oven is used mostly for storage."

"I'll never tell. But, since we have time before the tasting, I think I'd like to go for a walk on the beach this morning; the weather seems to be in our favor," Hazel said. "What say you? Want to come along?"

"Only if you don't do any impersonations or try and sing me a tune."

"You are more like your grandfather every day."

"I'll take that as a compliment. And, there're hot buns under the napkin next to the pot. I can't walk without sustenance."

"Fine. Now leave me to my morning ablutions. I'm a lot slower than you to pull myself together."

"In an hour then." Ellis exited through the adjoining door, careful not to slosh coffee on the frosted bun, but just as the door closed, she heard a faint and a very croaky rendition of *Don't be Cruel*.

Chapter 12

Nearly an hour later, Ellis sat on her bed brushing crumbs off her phone as she sent *xx's* and *oo's* to Artie. Her grandmother had rightly suspected Ellis was having cold feet, but it wasn't as clear-cut as that. She had blindly married a handsome and personable and silver-tongued lawyer, never once suspecting the real Walter until it was almost too late to save her self-esteem. But in truth, she was still naïve, still craving what she felt her grandparents had enjoyed, even though now there was a niggle of doubt about them. Beyond that, and perhaps just as important, she had naively believed Artie's mother would warm to her with time. It was obvious the woman had strong opinions, but not until Ellis had upped the date for the ceremony, had Marilyn begun to nitpick the many details that Artie had apparently been spoon-feeding her so that she would feel included. Ellis's gut told her there was something besides her divorce that was eating at the woman, and how could someone who'd birthed such a fine man, be so damned annoying anyway. Maybe pillow talk was the right next move after all. Ellis stared at Artie's face, his green eyes and full lips and all the heart emojis she'd saved on her phone. Finishing her coffee, she pondered her grandmother's suggestion. Within moments, she was conjuring other bed-related ideas to share with him, but then to her embarrassment, found herself wondering how many more marital tips her grandmother might be keeping to herself; not the kind of thing Ellis had ever intended to discuss, but then…the look on Gran's face when she was talking about that tango dancer. Wow! Ellis was beginning to think the put-together Hazel Mowry was quite something in spite of her age. Putting her empty cup on the tray, Ellis placed it on the desk identical to the one next door. In truth she liked Gran's room best—bigger, bolder, brighter is what she'd texted to Artie. And she'd never gone for that before, painting their cottage a soft opal shade, which in different light could look either white or blue. But of course, nothing was ever going to be the way it was before. She was suddenly being schooled in ways to think outside the box and from a woman she surmised was hiding something big. Ellis's mind was so mired in things she didn't know or hadn't known, that all she could be sure of right this moment, was her own body tingling in anticipation of returning home. Early mornings were their special times, and at this very moment Artie might be bent over his makeshift desk, a coffee in one hand and a sharpened pencil in the other, trying to make sense of a latest idea for her parents' store. It was an easy leap from that image to the summer months ahead and the way he'd look working in the yard in his coveralls and boots, or when it was too hot, shorts and his Patriots tee shirt stretched damply across his muscled chest. For all her jitters, she was grateful their meeting hadn't happened right away. She would've been too much of a mess back then to appeal to a guy who'd had his pick of the many available hometown girls. The year of celibacy and contemplation had done her good, and when they finally did meet, she was ready. And, Artie had been a rare find even in her limited experience with relationships: solid and warm from the very beginning. With her trust levels bottomed out in some imaginary hell, they had taken it slow, but as soon as they'd become close enough to live together and have the talk about important and intimate topics like invitro—for that was the route she'd more than likely have to go—her heart was more than ready to love again. And for all this new fretting, she knew how to package all his attributes into neat and tidy compartments: the way in which he handled his business, his dealings with her parents, his affection and respect for Gran. And the way he took care of a home that wasn't even their own, a thought that never failed to remind her of the way he looked hauling and hefting small boulders or hoisting rain gutters, or even an axe if need be, and all of it way beyond sexy after living with a desk jockey. Artie would often pick her up and lay her on the bed as though she weighed nothing at all. She felt heat crawl up her neck at the mere mental image of what it would be like after they were formally wed and spending those hours back here in the suite with the king-size bed, and the morning after, breakfast in bed until it was time to check out and not a second before. She had to practically will herself to put those thoughts away or she'd be spending the next few hours holed up with her phone and driving Artie crazy on the other end. She went into the bathroom and washed her hands, fluffed her hair and put on fresh lipstick, anything to keep from tormenting herself with more bedtime stories. Besides, right now she was positive her grandmother was trying way too hard to appear happy. Ellis threw her jeans jacket over her shoulders and reached for the handle on the door hoping her grandmother would feel more like her old self once she was back in her own home. And then Ellis thought, maybe coping and putting on a good face was another of those Beane anomalies, as if all the women in their line were meant to accept hard times only. *No more,* she thought as she walked through to the adjoining room; there had to be happier times ahead.

Chapter 13

Once outside, the morning seemed to be an extension of the lovely afternoon before, though the wind was far more bracing. Ellis put her arm around her grandmother's shoulder as they made their way down the path to the beach. "Are you warm enough?"

"Yes, even though I look like a puffed-up penguin," Hazel replied. "Good thing this was in the car."

"You look just fine."

"You'd say that no matter what."

"I did a lot of thinking earlier about that doormat issue, and you're right, I'm way better than that."

Hazel smiled. "That's my girl, and I'll back you up, you have to know that. We're all here for you."

"I know, Gran," Ellis said. "Let's head over to that flat boulder where you can sit while I take a few more pictures.

Hazel removed Ellis's arm, which was accidentally preventing her from walking properly. "At least the warm sun helps my achy knee," Hazel said. She'd probably turned it too hard when she'd tried that one intricate tango move, the only one she'd had time to remember. "When your granddad used to walk me through some of his building sites, he always said that when we got old, we'd need duct tape and spackle to keep our bodies intact."

"That's the weirdest and funniest thing you've ever told me about him."

"Makes sense, right—tape up the joints and trowel away the lines." Hazel laughed and broke off to her right where her bravado suddenly propelled her toward a foolish outcome. She was wearing the heavy-soled shoes again, and her tight twirl almost ended in a disastrous dump in the dirt as her toe hit a stone. "I should stick to knitting," Hazel offered.

"I wish I'd seen more of your dancing while Gramps was alive."

"We had our moments, but between us girls, I never told him about the tango. That was my private thing."

"Well, I'm not sharing it with Mom...."

"Exactly!"

"Did you like it, the tango I mean?"

"What little I learned, which wasn't much at all because the steps were complicated. I might have taken it more seriously if I'd been a little less self-conscious...it's a terribly intimate form of dance. And back then, I didn't have the words to explain it." She also had no way to explain how the dance is performed using a silent language with the eyes doing all the talking and the body conveying the heat-seeking messages.

"You must have told Sloane."

"Trust me, I wanted to, but they'd already left on their honeymoon. Besides, John had told her during the reception that he was going to propose, and it seemed so careless to be down there all by myself at that hour, so even after they returned, I was too embarrassed to say anything." And of course, something did happen, Hazel thought, and that something was a powerful aphrodisiac.

"And then, as they say, life happens when you aren't looking, or some such thing, and John was working day and night and it wasn't long before we had Janet to think about. By the time we got our crazy lives sorted out, the dynamics had changed and we saw less and less of them. They wanted children and couldn't get pregnant, and then because of Mike's work, they moved out of state for a few years. It wasn't until much later, that we found out he'd been lying to her about his job and a few other things that aren't important to this conversation. But I've always felt that the stress of living with that type of man was in part, what caused her cancer."

"Do you really believe that?"

"Some say stress is the precursor of many diseases."

"I've heard Mom say that too, but I've never paid much attention."

"I certainly never did when I was your age, but it's not

something to pooh pooh at, believe me.

"But as for Sloane, by the time they moved back to Maine and were living in Portland, things between us had changed somehow and I remember thinking we'd missed a step somewhere and I couldn't figure out where. And by then, Mike was different too. Who knows, maybe he was having an affair like your grandfather thought. I felt it was something else entirely, but then there were a lot of things I didn't know about Mike during that time."

"Do you think she was too embarrassed and that's why she disconnected?"

"I never thought of it that way; it makes sense in hindsight, Hazel said. "When we did get together on the rare occasions John felt like driving down to Portland for a dinner out, or to have them at our place, there was an obvious tension between her and Mike. He seemed patronizing and Sloane wasn't herself and John stopped wanting to be around them. I couldn't blame him, but I missed the friend I knew was hiding in there somewhere. Like you would Jeanie if she suddenly disappeared from your life."

"I can't imagine that happening at all. But you and Sloane obviously became close again."

"I honestly can't tell you how much time passed, but thankfully we'd found our way back to the way we'd always been, and well before I found out about the cancer.

Of course, by then, a dance of any kind was the last thing on my mind."

"She must have been awfully young when she died."

"March of '84, just after her forty-third birthday. And it hits me each anniversary as if it just happened." Hazel thought of the news articles tucked away. Why she'd kept such tangible proof of what came next, she couldn't say. Unless, of course, this visit to the Colony was all preordained as some prophets and priests liked to say.

"I'm happy to listen if there's more you feel like sharing."

"I've never known how to justify some of the more painful memories with the fact that she deserves the honor of never being forgotten. None of what she went through had to happen in the way it did. We knew she was going to die, but she wanted with all her heart and the energy still left, to die with dignity, which meant at home, in her own bed, surrounded by those who loved her. He took that away from her, and I haven't been able to forgive him that. It's not very Christian of me, I know, but it's a fact. Sloane suffered something awful toward the end. And, it didn't have to be that way, but Mike wouldn't listen." Hazel said. "And not for nothing, lots of people including my own mother, whispered the word cancer in those days, as if it could be catching or some such nonsense."

"And I thought Mrs. Granger was the crazy one with

her reaction to the word divorce," Ellis said.

"She's certainly a throwback, but I'm sure she's not the only one out there. But as a result of all those hushed-up attitudes, no one really talked about how to cope with cancer, and we didn't have options and alternative treatments or anything near what they do now.

"And you have to realize when Sloane was diagnosed, the first point of attack was surgical, a radical mastectomy. Next came chemo, which was nothing like what they've discovered in the last thirty years."

"So, basically, she was screwed from the beginning."

"That's a bit harsh, but yes, her situation was beyond bleak," Hazel said. "But in true Sloane form, once she'd healed enough to be able to move around easily, she had me over to her house to show off her scar; actually, she *made* me look."

"I don't think I could've handled that."

"Well, you had to know Sloane to appreciate the bravado. She'd always had the kind of figure you'd see in a fashion magazine, but on that day, she teased about looking like a model who posed in men's suits with slick-backed hair because now her own figure had become boyish, at least from one angle. She was the most unselfconscious woman I'd ever known, just stood there turning from side to side showing me the difference," Hazel said.

"She must have been one brave lady."

"She really was, and more than that, she had heart and the most amazing capacity to show love, something almost beyond the pale considering the way she might have turned out. She'd had a difficult upbringing, and up until her illness, she powered through everything.

"The long, deep pink scar was on the outside, but the worst ones were buried when she died, and I may be the only one left alive who knows what they were."

"Oh Gran."

"I know. But she'd always been far braver than me, and even during that last March, she was still making plans, getting the most out of her time. So many women didn't make it back then, but things are different now, and there are long-term survivors living all over the country because of new research and all the support groups."

"Where does Mike come into all this?"

"I'm embarrassed to tell you, but right up until the very end, John called Mike an arrogant prick."

"Kind of like *he who shall not be named*?"

"What on earth....?"

"I know you read Harry Potter."

"Ah, now I get it, the clothing brand."

"I was just hoping to make you smile for a minute; she was so lucky to have a friend like you."

"I always wished I could have done more. She was so

125

clear about everything. Your grandfather tried to warn me that I was too invested in their lives, but it was impossible for him to understand. I'm not sure men are equipped for that type of friendship, but maybe it's different these days."

"Artie's really close to Chad Corbishley, you know, his best man. Sometimes I think they gossip as much as Mom."

"At least he has someone he can talk to; John never had time for that kind of male bonding. I guess Mike didn't either, but love didn't give him the right to override Sloane's wishes." Hazel heard the bitterness in her voice. "I sound horrible, don't I?"

"You sound like someone who grieves deeply."

"If only he hadn't taken her to New York. It was a last-ditch effort that she went along with because she couldn't bear the idea of hurting *him*. Deep down, no matter how much I hate to admit this, Sloane knew exactly what all this was costing her, and she wouldn't have taken pleasure in knowing any of her friends have felt as I have all these years. But in the end, the treatment was killing her faster than the disease," Hazel said.

"You've been holding that in a long time, haven't you?"

"And it still breaks my heart," Hazel said. "I have to concentrate on some of the more positive memories while

I'm here or I don't know what I'll do."

"Then let's talk about something happy, like her cake."

There was pity in Ellis's eyes, a look which caused Hazel to rearrange her own face. "That's easy—over-the-top gorgeous! Tiered, with rose buds on each one and all of it trimmed in what looked like pearls. I do remember that it had started to list to one side, maybe from the heavy wedding topper, you know, the bride and groom dolls. I'm guessing they don't do that anymore?"

"Not on our cake anyway."

"I think mine's still buried somewhere in one of the umpteen boxes I put in storage although I don't know what I intended to do with it. I've gotten rid of a lot of memorabilia, but admittedly, our generation were serious hoarders: wall posters, ticket stubs, satin ribbons attached to trophies, letter sweaters or just the letter. Menus. You name it, and we probably collected it."

"And we're so opposite."

"And that's a very good thing." Hazel felt her heart quicken at the thought of the cassettes that had replaced 8-track and the music she'd acquired when there was an opportunity: the music of the dance that had laid claim to her heart when everyone else was still listening to blues or rock and roll. It was all packed away now and out of sight while John was alive. Often, when she was alone and Janet had just been put down, Hazel would listen to the yearning that emanated from a musician's classical guitar and imagine Eduardo. He became her fantasy—when too tired to think, too drained of anything, even her breast milk. Without that escape mechanism, her relationship with John could have become broken before it had a chance to solidify properly; it was not in her nature to be compliant on all things. Her husband loved her, she knew that without a doubt, but work and career would always take precedence over everything else.

"Will you stay on at the store after your wedding?"

"Believe it or not, Artie and I have been talking about buying Dad out; not right away, but soon enough to allow them to travel. They've been dying to go to Florida for the winters."

"Now it's my turn to gape."

"I know, but I've discovered how much I like what I'm doing, so much better than office work and being in front of a computer every day. I want to shake things up and make the space sing a little, something appealing to the tourists as well as the guys who already hang out there and tell stories, and pretend they don't notice the girl who crews for *Balmy Days*. Stories, as you've already pointed out are Mom's specialty. But I'm not like her, so I have to use other ways to try and make it work."

"My daughter's specialty has helped put money in Linden's pockets too, so I really shouldn't be so hard on her."

"And where else would they all congregate during the day so close to the waterfront without having to spend much money?" Ellis said.

"You're probably right, but do the numbers, please. If people aren't spending money, you'll go under pretty quick, even if Artie keeps up with his construction business."

"We've talked it out and I know you're right. And Mom and Dad have promised not to let me fall off the deep end."

"John would have been proud; he always knew you were creative."

"He would have loved this, are you kidding!"

"I'm also sure Artie's up for the challenge."

"He's the best, Gran, really."

If asked, Hazel would always be able to come up with ample descriptions about the men in all their intertwined lives—fathers, husbands, lovers. But for Sloane, there were not enough words, or enough years to put away the pain and heartbreak she had endured at the hands of various men, beginning with her own father who had turned out to be a mean closet alcoholic. No one but Hazel had known—and not until they were in their mid-teens—that the upstanding Mr. Harmon had molested his own daughter until she was old enough to fight back. And saddest of all, no one would have believed it back then. From what Hazel could recall, there weren't any laws in place to protect a child; perhaps Harmon would have received a slap on the wrist or maybe even a weekend in jail, but it would have been Sloane's word against his. And Ethyl Harmon with all her fancy ideas, would have been too humiliated even if she suspected the truth, to corroborate Sloane's story. And perhaps more afraid than anyone detected, to stand up to him. But women were fighting back now, and Hazel only had to watch the news to know what would have happened to that despicable monster in this day and age.

"If you show me how to use that phone of yours, I'll take some pictures of you with this great backdrop and a few of the hotel exterior with you standing in front so that you can show your folks. With the season about to start, they haven't had much time to spare, but this way, they'll get a better idea of what to expect here, and who knows, maybe if you can find time to manage the store for a day or two in between all this wedding stuff, Janet might talk your dad into an overnight before the summer crunch," Hazel said. "And, one other thing. I suggest strategizing about Marilyn Granger."

"How?"

"If it were me, I'd try to make her feel a little more important, at least for Artie's sake, give her something she can do that won't exactly put her in charge, but will help you out in the long run. Something like addressing envelopes or going with you to pick out flowers or favors. Then, it'd be easy to show your gratitude by taking her to lunch with your mom." Hazel said. "Or if you like, we could throw one of those lunches like I used to do for the visiting firemen, as John liked to call his favorite clients passing through on their way to Bar Harbor."

"You wouldn't mind all that fuss; Marilyn can be testy enough to be a real pain in the ass."

"I'd fix something special on Mother Mowry's plates, which you're set to inherit as long as you promise not to save them just for the holidays. And I still have some really fine wine hidden away from when I threw Millie a birthday party.

"Janet won't have to cook a thing, just bring a dessert," Hazel said. "Besides, I was trained by the best on how to deal with testy."

"Please don't tell me that's another Beane thing."

"Let's just say Midge could be the ultimate challenge, but she'd appreciate my doing what she'd never been able to, because first of all she never had anything quite as fine as Mother Mowry's dinnerware, and second, because she truly disliked cooking," Hazel said. "But she did dig politics, which isn't a bad quality."

"Not that again."

"It wouldn't hurt to put out some lawn signs when the time comes or drive some of us old fogies to the polls, and I can put you in touch with our local committee when you're ready."

"I'll think about it but not till after the honeymoon."

"Are you sure you wouldn't like a short trip abroad, maybe visit some of our old haunts?"

"Monhegan awaits, Grannie; it's one of our special places."

"Don't call me Grannie or I'll change my mind about everything."

"Truce!"

"Let's get back up to the hotel then and pack up our things; Portland also awaits... remember?"

Chapter 14

Within the city of Portland, there's an area known as the Old Port: cobblestone streets, quaint boutiques, tucked-away restaurants, gift shops, small hotels and art galleries, and as Hazel always said, there was something for everyone. Today, however, she was being held hostage in a third-floor room without so much as a peek of the working waterfront or anything close that might have made the stuffy space more bearable. It was small and dull and crammed full of boxes with all things bridal. The vents hissed and pinged as pipes rebelled within the old building. When they'd set out for Portland earlier, she hadn't a clue of what passed for a salon and fitting room these days, and for Ellis's sake once they were inside, Hazel had held her tongue. This loft space was a far cry from old Mrs. Waring's dining room in Boothbay Harbor where light filtered in through triple-hung windows and fell gently over her time-worn loveseat where guests could watch her magic with a needle and thread. Hazel's memory was crystal clear about a particular fitting when Sloane was being measured and pinned, and Mrs. Waring's granddaughter was in the parlor across the hall practicing *Clair de lune* on the notoriously out-of-tune upright piano—a regular *Little Miss Muffet* squirming on a hard, wooden bench, Hazel had thought at the time. And now, here she was seated on an uncomfortable tuffet of her own: neither an ottoman nor a proper sized chair. And nothing but a narrow window to provide natural light. A walk might do her some good, Hazel thought hearing a screech of tires followed by a loud horn, but she also disliked the idea of running out on Ellis in case another opinion was needed. By the time she looked down on the street below, whatever little drama there might have been was over and done with, and she laughed at the absurdity of worrying about Ellis in the hands of a gaunt-looking seamstress who seemed incapable of harming anyone but herself. Instead of using the plump, round pincushion she had attached to her wrist, she had stuck a dozen or so straight pins between her thin lips and was waving others around between the pinched fingers of her free hand. *They can't all be like dear Mrs. Waring,* Hazel thought about to turn away from the window when she noticed a sudden change in the buildings across the street. And then, she saw the startled expression on her face reflected in the glass, and her hand flew to her mouth. "Oh my god!" She stood there, mesmerized, watching the brick near the top portion of the many conjoined buildings change from deep maroon to a fiery rose. Pigeons soon honed in on the sun's angle, lining up on wires and sills and narrow plaster ledges, and squinted against the glare in order to bask in the rays. *Had it been the same time of day?* The room was suddenly pregnant with the past—as if the Colony Hotel hadn't been enough, it was 1963 all over again. Eduardo filling her up and frightening her with her own desire. The scene so like this one: three floors of brick with its counterparts across the street. Walls of windows keeping watch over each other as if silent spies in a dystopian novel. Those windows and the cobblestones on the street below, painted by the heat warming everything within its radius, had been a reminder Hazel hadn't expected. *She had promised after all.* Promised Eduardo she would see him in Portland the Saturday following Sloane's wedding. How incomprehensible that seemed now, but still, Hazel kept her eyes peeled on those glaring windows. He'd lived in one of the many brick apartment buildings downtown, though the actual street eluded her. *This is nonsense.* "I'm going down for some air," Hazel finally called into the dressing room. "I'll meet you out front."

Once outside, she crossed the one-way street, enjoying the same warmth as the birds above. Within the hour, the angle would change again, and the Old Port would be filled with shadows. Unlike Kennebunkport, the tourists weren't as evident on this weekday afternoon, and it was too early for office workers to lock their doors, so both street and car traffic were light. When they were newly married, John flew solo on business trips that took him out of the Portland airport. And later on, when they were able, they'd come into the city for theatre performances or the occasional dinner with the Kaplans. But back then, John's presence had usurped any reminders that could easily be hidden within a small city's nightscape. There was no finding comfort in that now. *The chances she'd taken to see Eduardo again.* Whatever silly lie she'd told John about her whereabouts on that Saturday—perhaps a look at wedding dresses, or maybe china patterns. Both activities would have seemed plausible and enough to satisfy him, but that only lasted until she lied again, and she'd never been adept at lying in the first place since her forehead spotted beet red whenever she tried. And before a second month had passed, John recognized her 'tell' like any good poker player would, and she'd played her cards badly. They'd had a terrible row and she'd returned the barely worn engagement ring which had been passed down to him through his mother's family. It was still the most beautiful ring she'd ever worn and was designated for the girl Jake would one day choose to marry, and suddenly the thought of that not happening was almost too much to bear. *There's no rhyme nor reason in revisiting this,* Hazel thought as she searched the street for a store carrying anything to counteract an unforeseen bout of lightheadedness. Not having eaten a proper breakfast, even a candy bar would do. The overhead signs were difficult to read from a distance, and by the time she reached the red door at the corner, she was willing to take a chance that somewhere within the advertised odds and ends, she'd find something edible. A bell jingled as she walked in. The room was cluttered, and none of it useful to her even if she weren't in need of a lift: hanging mobiles, beads and books on astrology and bags of runes, and an open Ouija board on the counter. No sign of a clerk or candy or even one of those boxy glass-fronted snack dispensers that existed in so many other public places. A wooden chair supporting a fat orange cat was propped next to the side wall. Music was coming from somewhere behind a curtain. Hazel wanted to sit. The cat glared at her. "You could sit on my lap little guy, okay?" Petting an animal was supposed to be good for lowering blood pressure or some such thing, she thought. Not this animal. He hissed and flew off the chair and shot behind the curtain. "Can I help you?" The voice, Hazel noted, was as indignant as the face of the man she'd obviously interrupted from doing god knows what behind the curtain.

"Sorry, I just needed a moment to get my bearings," Hazel said.

"Should I call an ambulance?"

"Don't be silly; I'm just a little faint from hunger."

"I'm afraid we don't carry any food, unless you count these chocolate good-luck coins," he said, pointing to a box of round gold wrappers next to a chubby Buddha statue. "There's a very nice donut shop just down the street; don't suppose you'd like to take refuge there."

Hazel supposed that being of a certain age and looking her best made no difference to someone without manners. "Yes, I think I'd prefer that to a creaky chair and a cold stare any day."

"Well I never...."

She was out the door before he'd finished his sentence. The gall of the man, she thought, and then realized she might actually enjoy a coffee-to-go, and by her watch, she still had time before Ellis was expected to finish with her fitting. There had been a mix-up in the size and getting the dress to fit perfectly was going to be a challenge, which only made Hazel strengthen her resolve to never order anything online. And by the time she'd exited one building and walked into another only a short block away, she had reaffirmed her own love of hunting and pecking through the clothing stores, always looking for the best bargains. Once she had a tall, frothy and very sweet coffee concoction in hand, she made her way back toward Exchange Street, bypassing the door to the bridal loft and heading directly to a bench near the intersection that was now in full sun. It was the perfect spot to ponder—not shopping and its many rewards, but a latent vision of a tucked-away bedroom on a long-ago and very cold November afternoon. She remembered a country in mourning, which at the time she hadn't associated with the dizzying nature of her actions with Eduardo—seizing the day and all that. Continual agonizing images run on a televised loop and everyone in a state of shock. Hazel's mind was filled with the visions of dark veils, coats and stockings; the draped flag and the tiny salute, and the stoicism that no one watching from afar could maintain. And she and Eduardo were so much alive, still trying to dance to his favorite piece of music played on a bandoneon, which turned out to be like a squeezebox, she remembered while still keeping a watchful eye on the entrance to the bridal loft. All around her, ordinary people were going about their everyday routines, some offering a nod or a smile, at least the ones who bothered to look up from their phones. There were no cellphones back then, but there would likely have been more crowd chatter, unlike the silent and intermittent passerby. Now, she was simply left to her daydreaming to fill up the time. Draining the last drop of coffee, she was disappointed by the inertia that still pulled her back down; even high-test couldn't seem to budge what was ailing her. And as she looked around for someplace to lose the empty container, she sensed a telltale shift and hurriedness beginning to occur on all sides of her as the few anonymous people became larger groupings and filled the cross streets, the day cycling once again. She found a bin nearby and just as she tossed the cup, she spotted a couple exiting a jewelry store only steps away from the opposite corner. She watched them kiss, and then put a hand into each other's back pocket as they walked away, wrapped in their own world and as oblivious to prying eyes as only lovers could be. And she realized that with all this reflecting and daydreaming, she couldn't remember if she and Eduardo had dared reveal such a public display of affection given their circumstances, or if they'd even taken walks, though she doubted it. But the question nagged—was it only lust—as it always had whenever she had tried to make sense or justify her actions, and because the entire affair with Eduardo ended before she'd had enough time to find out. Or without ever knowing what they might have been like when exposed to the arc of their various moods, hour by hour, day by day, and how they might tolerate their waking selves, disgruntled from dreams or nightmares, or bedding down for the night surrounded by the futility of angry words. And of all the people she might have leaned on, leaning on Sloane back then had been out of the question. Weariness was setting in. Hazel wanted to go home. *Midge wouldn't be having any of this nonsense,* she thought as she walked back toward the salon. Her mother always had a way of cutting to the chase. And, given a chance in 1963, she might have said Hazel was about to make the wrong bed. The woman was no prude and having dealt with Hazel's father in such a precise manner, and mincing no words, she might even have encouraged Hazel to fess up to John instead of diddling with his emotions. After all, Hazel had offered the lame excuse when pushed, that she'd been too absorbed in the aftermath of the assassination and all the rest, to set a date. On the other hand, Midge might have said there was no future with someone with such a foreign background. How could Hazel even consider such a thing? Instead, Hazel had sought out Aunt Charlotte's advice. A spinster, maybe, but she'd lived long enough to understand how the forces of nature worked, and that Hazel would be passing up a life of supposed security if she spurned John. But in the end, it was Eduardo who'd made the choice for her, backing away before she ruined her life, as he'd pointed out in the only clear-headed moment when they weren't tangled up in the bedsheets. He'd convinced her he had nothing to offer, wounded her pride and kissed her goodbye. What would have happened had they met at a different time in their lives? Unsophisticated on many levels and oh-so-broke, he'd been smart enough to realize they hadn't stood a chance. And back then, Hazel had sorely lacked her mother's type of courage. So, after designing the correct excuses, offering a proper mea culpa followed by plenty of tears, she'd made John believe it had been cold feet only, which hadn't been a total lie, and they set the date for their wedding. It had been the right thing to do, of course, but even as they became parents and moved toward his dream of success, Hazel had kept a piece of her relationship with Eduardo from harm's way. He was hers alone to remember, and as the years passed, she'd been right. As predicted, John had remained true to his nature: solid, level-headed, a caring dad, a real provider, and ultimately, the kind of man other wives envied and other men wanted at their backs. Their marriage had been good, even great at times. It had been enough. *Until now*, she thought just as Ellis came out of the doorway.

Chapter 15

Bright clumps of flowers grew antithetically on and in between many of the solid granite ledges at Ocean Point. The delicate gardens amazed those who walked or drove by this choice spot along the boulders that allowed for one of the best views of the Atlantic Ocean as it nudged up to the rocky shore. And this spring the flowers seemed more prolific than ever. But after a weekend at the Colony, Hazel wondered if instead of flowers, which she had used to brighten her own condo entrance, she should have had a sign made—Hazel's Retreat—instead of the unit number. Many of the summer people had quirky names for their cottages, so it wouldn't look all that unusual. But she would design hers as a white-capped wave on a marine blue background, and perhaps a small sail in the distance. She had never once given any thought to such a thing, but then, it had been a lot of years since she'd been so emotionally wrung out; who knows where her mind would go next. And, good or bad, Ellis possessed a lulling, mellifluous voice that under the right circumstances, encourages a nap, and in Hazel's case, one had been needed. But as soon as Ellis's car pulled out of the driveway, Hazel took her suitcase into the bedroom and without unpacking it, got out of her street clothes, removed her bra and expanded her chest wall—freedom! Sloane, never far from her mind now, had shown such shameless courage when it counted at the worst time in her life, but in the '60s when so many women were going braless, Hazel hadn't had the guts to do so. Just like she'd avoided so many of the protests taking place at the time, even if she hadn't dodged the proverbial bullet as she'd let others believe. There was Janet after all. And though Hazel hadn't said when she'd had the chance, there were plenty of political injustices for Ellis and her like-minded friends to flush out. The pendulum had swung again, and *Roe v. Wade*, though settled law, was being challenged on all sides. Immigration policies were still on shaky ground, and even solid science was being disputed. It was no longer enough to cast a vote, which Hazel never failed to do. In this fast-paced media environment, it took calls and petitions and protest marches and watchdog groups to uncover the truths. And this generation knew how to use social media in a way none of Hazel's lot had even heard of. She felt her pulse quickening; she was just working herself up for no reason. And she was tired and agitated and that was a combination that could cause her to phone her friend Millie, the only other woman who thought as much about bras and their significance (or lack of) as

Hazel. Millie would have made much of the youthfully styled black number that matched the blue one Hazel had purchased for Ellis's wedding and was now lying on the bed with its underwires exposed. But Millie had a husband, and Fred liked his TV shows, and Millie's voice carried. Hazel did one of her arm exercises, and stretched slowly and deliberately, forcing herself to put politics on the back burner for the rest of the night. Then she put on something too cozy to agitate anyone: a nubby top she wore when doing serious cooking, paired with her elastic-waist pants and the pair of worn leather mules she liked the sound of as they slapped against her wooden floors.

"Enough," she said as she faced the full-length mirror. Too much time had already been wasted on anger and resentment. She had sounded quite preachy when she talked with Ellis about pent-up anger and its outcome, and yet Hazel was nearly strangled by it. And it wasn't going to get better any time soon…unless. On the way home, just before she'd dozed off, she'd remembered the two-thousand-year-old practice and the small bundle of dried white sage and sent up a note of thanks to June. She'd called it ritual alchemy and when Hazel moved to the new condominium and after they'd burned the sage and smudged the unit throughout, June had left an extra bundle for good measure, which Hazel had stashed in a dresser drawer among needles and pins and packets of buttons. *Now's the time for some of that goodness,* Hazel thought as she unwrapped the potent herb. But like anything else done right, it had to be performed the way June had shown her, a real ceremony that would act as a blessing by the time Hazel was finished: first, she had to get all of her thoughts on paper because that made them real; then, she'd burn the paper, releasing the never-before verbalized toll on her heart. And when the time was exactly right, she'd light the foul-smelling sage, smudge the unit again, and be done with it! She began to laugh at the thought of them like a couple of throwbacks to a tie-dyed era, when in actuality she and June were both a bit staid. But maybe not too much longer. Hazel thought that tomorrow she might go to the storage unit and dig out the box of tapes and play the heart-tugging music as loud as she wanted before it was too late—the realtors had begun showing the unit next door.

Could have used the stupid sage when old Ethyl died, Hazel thought as her mind rewound to the days before her own wedding when Mrs. Harmon died of a stroke. There Hazel was without a maid of honor and wanting more than anything to tell Sloane about Eduardo instead of being angry because her absence would make the winter wedding more uneventful than it had already become. In the end, Hazel had convinced a cousin to stand in on such short notice, and Sloane had skipped the fray at the funeral home viewing and attended the new Mr. and Mrs. Mowry's small but tasteful wedding reception and had her picture taken with Hazel, which had also been tucked away with the cherished tapes. But best of all, she and Sloane had concluded during the many toasts, that Mrs. Harmon was going to be joining Mr. Harmon in a place apropos of their daughter's childhood traumas.

Not everything had turned to crap. That was Hazel's recollection of John's words when she'd thought everything to do with their wedding was about to hit the fan. He was a most unusual man she reminded herself, and not for the first time. He'd accepted her no matter what and to this day, she believed she'd done her penance and been the kind of wife he'd imagined when he first proposed. But then, tucking the sage into her pocket, she noticed her face in the mirror, a small, sardonic smile changing her expression. She turned away and reached into her closet for the album because once she was finished writing the letter, she planned to spend some quality time reacquainting herself with the girls in blue. And if she were very lucky, she'd find face of the man who some might have thought foreign and exotic somewhere among the sea of ordinary ones.

Taking her treasures to the living room, she put them on her desk and went to the kitchen for a much-needed glass of red wine to help loosen the tension she'd carried from the harbor to the Colony and back again. Had anyone asked why all of this was so important, Hazel wouldn't be able to say, but as she poured the wine, she noticed the kitchen window across the room had just turned a melancholic blue-gray, which then urged a sigh from her chest that could have been heard next door, had anyone been living there. Each day when she awoke, she gave thanks that no one had bought that unit—yet; it was difficult enough to adjust to shoe-box spaces without sacrificing other privacies as well. Sometimes, she got the tiniest of thrills from slamming a drawer or turning the TV up an extra notch, just for the pleasure of being able to while the unit remained empty. Childish yes, but satisfying nonetheless, and without any twinge of guilt, Hazel now banged the palm of her hand on the wall that would have mattered.

Tired words from the past curled around the ones she now wanted so badly to purge on paper, adding them to the ones she'd already written after Sloane's illness had taken over: *You were the rock and spirit we all gravitated toward and the hero we all needed. Our hopes and dreams were on you to survive, as we couldn't imagine our lives without you.*

Hazel went into the living room and ran that same palm over the honed wood of her antique Queen Ann desk before opening the drawer. She had learned from John whose creative genius would sometimes cause him great angst, that writing spaces were important. He'd rail against the unfairness when the muse failed to appear, and even against her if she tried to cajole him from his inner demons. Coming to grips with the weight of his responsibilities—the perfection needed in order for buildings to maintain their integrity—hadn't been an easy process for her. And she'd often offered platitudes that fell short of their mark. But she never balked at his need to have that certain space all his own with which to create the promises he envisioned for his clients. And there was that word again...promises, and she rolled it on her tongue and mingled it with the taste of wine she had just sipped, and then, she put the stemmed glass on a coaster.

Removing two pristine sheets of paper from the drawer, along with a souvenir pen from Italy, Hazel sent up a silent plea; she was unaccustomed to praying for anything, but to her limited knowledge, there didn't seem to be any other way to forgive Mike. And that was key to the success of this ritualistic endeavor.

She slipped off her mules, studying what was left of the twilight view and the curling waves tipped with the lavender of evening, and mentally rehashed the weekend because it was easier than getting down to the business at hand. It occurred to her as she pondered the changing sky, that she may have become rusty at hating.

Words that she had been waiting all this time to voice,

with or without paper, would not come forth. She nibbled at the pen's Murano glass tip and subconsciously began jotting things down willy-nilly, another one of those small rituals to get the juices flowing. She paused for a sip of wine, looked at the paper in front of her, only to find that what she'd actually been notating was a list of secret desires which could only have been spawned by her continual reimagining of Eduardo's Portland apartment.

She stood and fluttered the now too-warm top away from her chest, her better intentions fluttering into a temporary oblivion.

This behavior was ridiculous; when was the last time she'd had any kind of sex, let alone steamy? Like a nervous tick, she began fiddling with her rings, twisting them around the pinky and index fingers of her right hand, the weight of the gold between her fingertips almost like a meditation, since she'd never learned another way to clear away her doubts. She didn't know what John would think about the Italian jewelry assuming this kind of power, or what he'd make of all this hullabaloo over a luncheon for Ellis either, but rather than sit here all flummoxed over that silly list, Hazel dug out her social calendar and began circling possible dates. John was too much of a pragmatist to have worked himself up as Hazel was doing; these worries were strictly emotional and didn't count. *That may be so, but*...her stomach rumbled so loud that it was as if he'd decided to interrupt her before she could finish her thought.

Between her hunger and her angst, she now couldn't decide whether or not to take another stab at a list having nothing to do with the luncheon, but the pros and cons of trying to find a once-upon-a-time lover of little renown whose greedy eyes had once inspired her to take chances. The sage taunted her lack of purpose and she put it back in her pocket and slid her feet into her mules and went back to the kitchen. She hated the idea of being so indecisive, but she was suddenly famished. There was pea and ham soup in the freezer. Dinner would be an easy fix: a bowl of soup, a handful of crackers and more of the cheery red wine. "How bad can that be?" Hazel laughed at her imitation of one of her favorite TV chefs, thinking of all the times she'd said this aloud when fixing a lonely meal. *Laughter aids digestion,* she thought as she was taking the soup from the freezer drawer. She placed the container in the microwave, then poked her index finger at the Defrost icon. The small appliance came to life with a hum and a whir, the heavy glass turntable emitting a soft bump as the tiny wheel hit a misalignment for no apparent reason other than it happened after each time it was removed for washing. She stood there, lulled by the inane musicality created inside a metal box until the hum overrode the intermittent bump, and a different sound filled the gap.

Her hips responded to an imagined tempo and began to move in a suggestion of intimacy, albeit without the fluidity she'd never possessed even in her youth, though Eduardo had done his best to change that.

What he'd done to her and how he'd done it, flooded her brain and went beyond anything she'd conjured in the ballroom. Thoughts buried so deep she'd forgotten their truth until this very moment. When had she crossed the line, she wondered, from proper widowed matron to passionate girl? Had the Colony unleashed a hidden side of her that once exposed might disturb the viewer as much as those paintings hanging in the hotel lobby.

And more importantly, what was she going to do with the rest of her life? As if in answer, the microwave beeped its last note and the room filled with a dull silence, the sort of quiet she knew couldn't be filled by routine movements. While she'd been waiting, a black void had stained the kitchen window, leaving her reflection to mock her failed performance as well as the face she'd grown used to.

Hazel turned away, embarrassed by her foolish notions, and removed the bubbling soup. *Fine dining, it's not.* "But good enough," she muttered as she brought it to the counter and ladled the soup into a blue pottery bowl. Then, picking up an heirloom soup spoon bearing her mother's initials, she began what would be the easiest part of what was left of the evening.

The turntable may have stopped, but the unrealized yearnings would continue to go round and round like a carousel without an off switch, each memory rising up or down on its own. *Eduardo.*

Chapter 16

Rain poured from the gutters; the noise exaggerated by the aluminum material and interrupting what Ellis supposed would qualify for pillow talk, though it didn't seem to be working.

Artie tossed aside his half of the cotton sheet, and turned on the light in order to search the window panes for any signs of a leak. "But we can't go meddling like that, Ell," he said above the din.

"I know, but I can't just let it go. Can't we at least try to find him?"

"Personally, I think you're asking for trouble, but then as you always point out, I'm just a guy."

"You proved that quite nicely last night," she said, rolling over as he got back in under the covers, and showing him her gratitude.

"Not going to change my mind."

"Are you sure?" She stroked him until he groaned.

"Totally unfair," Artie gasped. "But who knows, I *could* be persuaded."

"I'll try to make a good case then," she said as she put her lips to his to stop any further conversation.

A half hour later, Artie threw his legs over the side of the bed and ran his hand through his hair. "Geez, Ell. I'm gonna need a nap before I go to work."

"Not my fault."

"Like hell it isn't," he teased. "But if your crazy idea backfires, I'm the one pleading the fifth!"

"Fair enough," she replied. "And since we didn't get very far on that seating chart last night..."

"And whose fault was that?"

"No matter, we'll work on it tonight." She hadn't played fair, she knew. He'd been so happy to see her and after telling him all about Hazel's mystery man, Ellis had brought him cake in bed as a treat, and the rest was as they say, history. "Do you have to leave so early?"

"If I'm gonna get the interior finishes on that job over on the east side; otherwise, I'll be putting in overtime and you won't like that at all."

"I'll go make coffee then."

"Thanks, babe, and make enough for a thermos too, okay?"

"Yes, my lord. Any other requests?"

"Sassy wench." He winked before closing the bathroom door.

"Better watch out, King Arthur, or I'll poison your gruel."

"Can't hear you!"

Love of my life, joy of my bed, a funny phrase her grandmother's friend Millie had said on more than one occasion. She giggled; it was hard to imagine the seventy-five-year old, lanky Fred Treadwell being the joy of anyone's bed. Then she caught herself—what did these older women know that she didn't.

The rain continued to slap the window, magnifying what she was certain was going to be a very gloomy Tuesday morning. It had been a sweet return home and Artie had done all that he could while she was away. A house of their own was in their future—with a fireplace and a shower built for two—something they found both fun and sound practice, at least that's what they'd convinced themselves whenever the opportunity rose. But even this wonderful daydream couldn't remove the image of her grandmother, sitting on the hotel bed trying so hard to disguise whatever she'd been contemplating. Ellis could hardly bear the idea that her grandmother carried around the weight of so much sadness.

While she waited for the coffee to brew, Ellis reached for her computer. Googling an Eduardo or Edmund or Edward Roca might or might not lead anywhere, but she had to try. She certainly didn't think he'd been a household name among followers of Latin music or her grandmother would have known, but then Ellis thought she could be wrong about that as well. She had never followed any of the TV reality shows that featured dancers, but the reality here was that this man was old, like her Gran and probably no longer involved with any dance studio.

Search algorithms had a will of their own and in the end, all she could find was an organization for retired dancers. She made notes and closed her computer and joined Artie in the bathroom.

"No, no, no...I'm already late," Artie said as she snuggled up behind him. "A tad sex-crazed aren't we on this fine rainy morning."

"Just showing my appreciation. And by the way, I found an organization for retired dancers but nothing more. Any suggestions?"

"Yeah. Leave it alone."

"Try again."

"Ell, how would I know anything about dancers or their studios?"

"I'm going to ask Millie; at least she won't give me a hard time."

"Perfect, now you can quit badgering me."

Ellis ignored the smirk, "She's the only one I'd trust and I'm positive she'd find this right in her wheelhouse."

"You mean she's been harboring secret fantasies about tango dancing?

"Now you're just being fresh," she said pinching his butt.

"Ouch! Can't you see I have a blade in my hand?

"I'll let you know how I make out," Ellis said removing her thin cotton nightshirt and stepping into the shower stall.

"You do that, deah."

"Last chance."

"Just wait till I get home tonight."

"Promises, promises."

"I'm outta here before you get any more ideas." Artie said. "Anything else you need me to do?"

"Fill in the crater in the driveway?"

"Just as soon as it dries out."

"Any chance the most eligible bachelor on the peninsula knows anything about Latin dancing?" Ellis said from behind the curtain.

"Why don't I just drop in and ask him one of the dumbest questions he's ever been asked."

"At least find out what he thinks about the music for the reception...paleese!"

Artie peered around the shower curtain and said, "You know, you're getting awfully hard to please."

"Out!" Ellis pulled the curtain closed and said, "Mark my words, if you don't leave right this minute, you will be late for work." They had more than enough chemistry between them, but her mind had already switched gears. "What's happening with your sister?"

"Still not sure, but if my mother has her say, Sheila will be there with or without her snob of a husband."

"Maybe without is better, but don't tell them I said so."

Artie stepped back, shaking his head as always and kind of wishing he could be late. "I'm gone; see you later." He had more on his mind than Sheila; his mother had found another sore spot to pick at and he didn't know how to handle it.

~

Over at Ocean Point, Hazel awakened to the sound of rain lashing against her bedroom window, as well as a residual image of small horses going up and down shiny poles. She refused to even budge from the bed until she heard the signal indicating the coffee was ready. She'd had a restless night and the only thing she had actually accomplished before turning out the light, was the June 1st date and a list of ideas for what she considered an elaborate luncheon. Rolling over, Hazel stared at the window, willing the rain to stop and for something else to fill its place; she was far too fixated on the night before, and she had no clue how to handle the raw nakedness of the feelings she'd exposed, which only showed her how far she'd taken her little fantasy. Finally, hearing the sound of four high-pitched beeps, she bypassed the Moroccan dressing gown in favor of a practical waffle-textured cotton one that had come as part of a gift bag from a trip she could barely remember. Slipping her feet into her mules, she headed for the kitchen, switching on each lamp as she went on through, which immediately transformed the gloom into a mixed salad of blues that she had artfully tossed together when she first moved to the complex. Her love of the ocean could be seen from every angle and was the perfect color scheme for an otherwise boring, open-plan unit. And perhaps the only thing she had going for her on this grainy-looking morning. The coffee smelled dark and rich, the way the beans looked when she first put them into the grinder, and knowing the wedding album was where she'd left it the night before, she filled an oversized cup hoping the strong brew would cut through the clutter of her mind before her emotions could devour yet another day. She had never thought of herself as this type of dreamer, and now it seemed that's all she was doing. But for the moment, she was determined to find the face of the man who might have changed the course of her life, even if it was so long ago it could hardly matter. She yanked on the belt of her robe. There was no getting away from it, everything about him now mattered, and without realizing, she placed the cup on the small table next to the window seat with more force than necessary, and droplets flew over her hand and onto the album cover. Before she could dot them dry with a tissue, the graying satin bloomed with dull freckles. Wedding albums like this were a thing of the past, and because the photos were irreplaceable, like those she'd already removed to show Ellis, the entire book of memories needed to be handled with care. Hazel took another sip of coffee and stared at the rain, willing Eduardo into being. Then she took off her shoes and tucked her feet into the dark blue throw at the end of the window seat and began her search. Within minutes she was back in the '60s, everyone looking young and vibrant. It was like going through an old class yearbook where everybody was frozen at whatever stage in life the camera had caught them. And no matter how many years passed, in her eyes this very special crowd would always be shouting with possibilities. It didn't matter that through time, many of the participants would have lost their hair or their waistlines or even their lovers and life partners. It was the continuum of life-affirming moments held in schools and churches and synagogues or even altar-less resorts. She gnawed on her lip. *You're laughing your socks off, right Sloane,* Hazel thought. She'd certainly taken this task to heart.

Hazel finished her coffee, contemplating what she had never thought to do before the trip to the Colony had made it necessary. Using her index finger as a guide, she traced it gently over each photograph, identifying each person whose name she remembered. *Everyone was so unassuming back then.* The bridesmaids, all in their twenties and needing little makeup other than mascara and lipstick, and for the wedding day, blue eye shadow, which had also gone the way of uncompromising girdles. In the front of the album, all of the girls in blue had been posed like a cascading waterfall with one girl on each stair, and by their expressions, totally unaware of their fashioned immortality. Hazel knew who'd been responsible for the creative shot of the groomsmen standing at the bottom of the stairs as if waiting to catch them, but she was certain Eduardo hadn't been able to control the way they mugged for the camera, their time-stamped haircuts as yet untouched by the gusting wind. She had no real memory of what had taken place to get the perfect lighting for the glamor shot of Sloane at the top of the stairs, but Hazel was certain it had been a long time before she'd been given the cue to pick up the train. "Of course!" she shouted at her reflection in the window. Old Ethyl had hung Sloane's gown out in the hall near the large window and well away from mascara wands and hair spray. It probably was a good idea, but at the time it seemed Ethyl was simply hollowing out a little more control over Sloane's big day. Hazel passed quickly over any photographs favoring Mike, except to reaffirm his resemblance to the 35th

President. In one of the panned shots, she spotted Midge in her best wool suit, seated next to Ethyl who must have just come inside after the formal family photograph, and still wearing her fox stole that had been so in vogue at the time. The lifelike eyes seemed to be imploring Midge to do something, but from the discomfort on her face, she had probably suffered through the proximity of the small beast until she could find someone else to talk with. *Blasphemy,* she would have said and Hazel, of course, had never accepted John's offer to buy either of them anything adorned with real fur, even before wearing pelts of any kind fell out of fashion. Although there was a particularly brutal winter when Hazel almost regretted those decisions. But as her eyes scanned the photos, she tried her best to put a name to the faces of the rest of the wedding guests, many of the girls from their high school in particular, who seemed to have tried making statements of their own by wearing either the popular pearl-buttoned sweaters and pencil skirts, fashionable A-line dresses ala Jacqueline Kennedy, or simple pastel colored sheaths, and all with a nod to the fall season. Hazel didn't remember plaid having been any part of her own wardrobe, but there seemed to be plenty of tartan in these photographs. Her mind began to lazily drifted over the pages until she had most of the harbor guests identified, and sometimes that was more about whether they were dancing or just standing in front of the long table that acted as the bar.

Studying the crowd, she could almost hear the din of their voices mingling with the rain continuing to patter against her favorite window. The rhythm had slowed from the earlier deluge, but the sound encouraged drowsiness. *Just two more pages,* she thought just before she bolted upright. A head of dark, wavy hair almost to the collar. *Eduardo?* So familiar and yet so hard to be certain and the man was turned away as if he was about to exit the room. She turned two more pages before she saw the same head of hair and definitely the same jacket, his attention now on the tug of his arm from a little girl with golden hair. *One of the flower girls, of course!* The next picture on the same page showed the little minx minus the wind-battled floral wreath, standing on Eduardo's toes readying for that unique big-girl dance, more than likely foisted upon him by the parent taking the photo. Whoever it was, might have been trying to make up for the child's earlier bad behavior, but in this photograph, she was visually all sweetness and light.

Hazel's heart did a little flip—he'd been hauled from obscurity by one endearing moment, and no matter what happened next, she knew he'd always be remembered through the same medium he'd taken at least some pleasure in. His features were remarkable, but then, he'd also been young at the time. And, those wonderful shoulders, she thought. Why is it that women never seemed to mention how sexy shoulders could be? She wouldn't have noticed that about him during Sloane's wedding, she realized, because naturally, she'd only had eyes for John, until he'd left her behind and changed the course of events forever.

Hazel's phone interrupted her reverie, but she was in no mood to talk to anyone just yet. The entire album had touched someplace deep inside her, and just as with the hotel, everything about reclaiming that day led back to Sloane. In her mind, Hazel could hear Sloane's voice: *forgiveness won't come if you won't let it.* Hazel knew when she was bested. She got up and went back to her desk and began to write the only way she knew how and with the words she'd put off for far too long.

Here goes old friend,

First, I spent this past weekend at the Colony Hotel, where I relived about as much as my aging brain could recall. I talked with you too, right out loud, like some crazy person. Do you remember the first time we went to Kennebunkport shopping? We never did find what we were looking for, but just for kicks, we stopped in at the Colony and wandered around trying to act like we belonged in such a grand place. Well, it's all still there, even the ballroom and that chandelier that had you in thrall. Unbelievably, you made your wish come true. And now, it's my beautiful granddaughter's turn to dance beneath the crystal chandelier with her handsome prince, which is how everyone thought of Mike back then.

My John has been gone a little over five years now. Janet, my dark-haired beauty, is now menopausal, but since you escaped such a fate, I hardly think you would empathize, but believe me, it hasn't been fun being around her. Ellis, my only granddaughter, is a true joy and so much a Mowry it's uncanny. She asked a lot of questions, but to do them all justice, would have taken more time away from her and the details she needed to finalize. And I would have had to explain everything — the nitty gritty of what brought you to the pinnacle of your once in a lifetime day; the strange relief after your father died, which was the only way you could have had a storybook wedding in the first place. And how awful it was to watch your mom lapping it all up as if you'd had a well-orchestrated life. Ha! We both know that ain't true. Sorry, I've just reverted to my snarky teenage self, and I needed that, trust me. I also felt it a duty to tell Ellis about your illness; after all, we women can't avoid things like check-ups. And, to this day, I struggle with my inability to help you as I'd promised, even though it was out of my hands. Did you understand? I try to imagine what it's like where you are, but like most of us down here, I don't have a clue or if you are keeping tabs on us or just floating around in some undisclosed fifth dimension headquarter. I'm still not sure I believe in the afterlife, but maybe you'd send a message so I don't screw up when my time comes. If there is a heaven, I'm pretty sure you're in it, so, if you are tuning in, you probably need to forgive me for my irresponsible behavior right after you guys left on your honeymoon. I won't bore you with the details but it started with a dance, a tango. Now I know you're laughing; I didn't exactly have great rhythm back then. Not that it improved over the years, but John was a fairly good dancer, and I guess I caught on enough to keep up with him, but I must confess my indiscretion. Yes, goody two shoes had a secret, and his name was Eduardo. Now I know you're rolling your eyes, so spare me the abuse of words I believe you'd say. You admired John like the brother you never had, and this other man sounds so foreign, isn't that what our mothers would have said at the time? Thank goodness that type of thinking isn't common in the context of my granddaughter's lifestyle. Anyway, you would have known him as Ed, your wedding photographer, though I doubt anyone but your mother paid attention to his full name. And I never asked him why he'd kept it from us—by then I was too far gone in my fantasy to think of it. Well, you wonder, what did I expect but that John would find out? Which of course he did, in a way. But only that I'd lied, not whom I'd lied about. I went to stay with Aunt Charlotte while I figured things out, and she sent me packing when she found out I'd missed my period. And by then, John had been worried he'd lost me forever. To my amazement, going back to that hotel with Ellis turned out to be both a blessing and a curse. I've begun to fantasize about Eduardo all over again, though in truth, given our ages, he may also be dead. Now I can't even imagine what you're thinking.

Hazel put down the pen and stood and rotated her neck and stretched her fingers out and did a few squats, a pretense only. Millie often said that Hazel was so disciplined, keeping up her routine at the Y, but in fact it was pain that motivated her. And yet, it was the knot in her soul that needed work, and there were no exercises for that. *Stalling won't change things,* she thought as she sat back down and began again.

This little missive isn't as easy as I thought it would be, especially since I can hear your voice as if it were yesterday — the way you talked about love, even after all you'd been through. You managed to find a way to keep your heart from freezing over, and you opened it again and again, no matter what slights or unhappiness you endured. But the voice I struggle with on each anniversary of your death, is when you called me from your hospital room in New York. "I'm coming home!" you'd said across the wire, loud and clear. The treatments had all but decimated your poor body and almost withered your soul. You'd been crying because you couldn't take any more, not even if they could perform miracles; you were done! I'd encouraged you to come home, against Mike's directives, and I was so thrilled to be the one to tell everyone the best news ever. Only the following morning, I received a different call. It was from your nurse. There'd been such unmistakable joy in your voice, an emotion one usually doesn't equate with ensuing death. I cannot remember the exact details the nurse gave me, which had something to do with the blood-brain barrier, and whatever it was, it had happened during the night, and you had died alone. Only then did he bring you home—in a plain pine box. But it gets worse.

Hazel saw the wet spot on the last line before she felt them against her cheeks. She had to push the page away to save it from the sobs that followed. She cried until she was spent, and then became defiant—she had one more thing to tackle. Walking back to the window, she picked up the album and opened it to the back cover where she had stapled the obituaries, and brought them to her desk where she tucked them in the drawer to burn along with the letter when she'd finally gotten everything off her chest. But even before Hazel looked at the words she almost knew by rote, her eyes began to fill all over again. Only this time, she refused to stop what had taken her so long to forgive.

I've tried for many years to justify everything Mike didn't do: no service to celebrate your life, no music or poems or flowers. If possible, he would have prevented any of us from even being at your grave. We—all of your attendants—defied him and brought small handfuls of your favorite flowers, and linked hands around your grave in further solidarity as we said what words we could, together, quietly. Even as Mike, supported by Leo, your least favorite brother-in-law, glared at us, we managed to toss our inadequate bouquets onto your casket as we said our final goodbyes. But no matter how hard and long I've tried, I fear I'll never forgive him for taking his own life when you had struggled so hard to save your own.

Suicides were not in their young lexicon, not the way they've now touched just about every walk of life in the twenty-first century. But it didn't make it easier for Hazel to handle the fact that Mike chose to end his life, cruelly, at Sloane's gravesite. But it was well past time for compassion, and writing this letter after such a long period of resistance was meant to heal her heart not break it all over again. Then she made the mistake of taking another look at the faded newsprint, and her anger flared anew. *How is it possible they'd allow such news to take up more space than Sloane's obituary?*

But what's done is done, she ruled using her fist as a quiet gavel. She had written honestly and from her heart;

it's what her dearest friend would have done in a similar situation. Gathering up the letter and the newspaper articles, Hazel tucked them into the drawer of her desk for safekeeping. She would have to wait for the smudging ceremony until after June 1st, or her guests might believe she'd been smoking pot while cooking up the special dishes she had planned. But right now, she needed to get organized for what she hoped would be a fantastic event. Sunday was just days away, and organizing meant starting with a solid menu first and then an intricately coordinated grocery list. *Not your first rodeo old girl,* she thought as she turned on the radio, rather loud even to her ears, but a classical station that would pour out cymbals and drums and up and down notes of the cello and all the instruments that might herald in a fresh start. While she listened, she dug through four of the five cookbooks she kept on the kitchen shelf; the Italian one wouldn't be necessary for this particular menu. All of her cookbooks had been spattered by something, some more than others, and all definitely bearing the signs of a little sauce here, and a lot of butter there, and even a dab or two of chocolate smeared against recipes she'd used as standbys for birthdays and anniversaries. She was better at baking than Ellis, but not as good as Janet and yet neither could hold a candle to the over-the-top fixings Hazel prepared through the years for every special occasion, not only for family, but when John needed to entertain clients. All that practice had turned her into a really good cook.

By the time she'd made all her selections and all the notes on timing them properly, because that too was a part of her success in the kitchen, it was past ten and too late to call her daughter about bringing dessert. *Time enough in the morning,* she thought as she turned off the radio. And in that new silence, she remembered the key she kept in the drawer used for plastic wrap and rubber bands, the key to the storage unit across town. She let out a breath of pleasure at the mere thought of having the tapes in her hands again. The idea of relearning the steps made her pretend-dance her way to the shelf with her cookbooks in hand, and then she turned off all the lights. Tomorrow would be a good day indeed.

Chapter 17

Hazel had practically worn out the first tape by the time Sunday rolled around. And even this morning, she'd been playing it non-stop until she realized she didn't want to have to explain anything to her guests and there would definitely be questions. It was not the type of music normally heard in their households, and she simply wasn't ready to share her love of it with anyone. Instead, she donned her imaginary hostess hat, and put the classical station on while she ran through the last-minute prep, remembering just how much she enjoyed the fuss and bother. She also had a sneaking suspicion that the tango music had misled her into thinking she hadn't slaved for hours to make sure everything was perfect, including the menu that she'd printed up and was now lying on the counter:

Appetizers ala Martha Stewart—White Zinfandel.
Mixed salad with pears, goat cheese and dried cranberries, topped with homemade dressing
Boneless spinach-stuffed chicken thighs—French vintage white wine
Homemade bread with olive oil for dipping
Lemon cream pie—Prosecco—coffee or tea

Hazel had planned it all out with Ellis in mind, choosing simple, but impressive dishes that she could make on her own if she chose. Hazel had gone a bit overboard, but this was about Marilyn Granger after all, which meant to Hazel that it was also about Artie. She knew that Ellis hadn't yet grasped the importance of combining mother and son when making certain decisions having to do with married life, but she would learn. Hazel had, and even though she'd smoothed it out for Ellis, Mother Mowry had a way of making her point of view known, just as Hazel was certain she had with Linden in those earliest years of her daughter's marriage. Maybe it was an unspoken rule, but whatever it was, Hazel knew they'd all get through it together.

The day had cooperated as if it too had been orchestrated by a wise weatherman. All morning, lobstermen had been pulling up their traps and herring gulls waited waterside on the ledges, or wheeled overhead waiting to pounce.

Hazel had left one of the windows cracked open to bring in the scent of the sea and while she rechecked her list, she listened to gull language as well as the rhythmic starting up and slowing down of heavy throttled engines, a cycle that was performed daily and was always music to her ears. Small waves were churned up by this morning's boats as they arrived one after another, each returning daily to their coveted patch of the cove, and each time a wave was lifted out of the water, it turned a bottle-green color just before coming ashore. The sounds had become an anthem to waterfront living and one she would never be able to live without again.

The pot buoys closest to the shoreline beyond her window were a gaudier red because of the slant of the sun at midday. Beyond those buoys, the sea was littered with a field that led all the way to Ram Island Light: light green with blue accents, yellow and white, and then blue and orange, until the last of the buoys disappeared into a milky yellow haze in front of the headland — all of them forming a sprouted garden of water nymphs.

It was an onshore breeze today and just cool enough that Hazel didn't need the air conditioning and perfect for her beige linen slacks and long-sleeve cotton sweater in seafoam green. She moved about comfortably on the beige flats she'd come to adore, and gave the living room and dining room a final once-over since her guests were due to arrive at any minute. Then, as she straightened the clasp on the pearls for which John had paid a king's ransom during one of his magnanimous moods, she remembered the last bit of gossip Janet had hurled at her during their last phone conversation. Where her daughter had learned such a ludicrous story was beyond Hazel, but rumor had it that Marilyn had worn her robust (Janet's word) pearls to her last doctor's exam and left them on to apparently enhance the boring and unflattering johnny-gown, which Marilyn said had given the exam a whole new meaning. All Hazel could think was that Marilyn had thought she'd look so alluring in the pearls she wouldn't have to pay attention to the rest, or Hazel wondered, was it perhaps that Marilyn's doctor was also the most eligible, middle-aged specialist practicing in Midcoast Maine.

But as Hazel stroked her own pearls, she thought if they got along well enough today, she might be able to ask Marilyn about the story. Then again, with her own warped sense of humor, Hazel figured she probably wouldn't be able to keep a straight face.

Checking her hair in the hall mirror one last time, she had one ear cocked for the sound of the little toot of Janet's Mini-Cooper, which would be followed by the crunch of tires on gravel from both cars. The aftermath of an overzealous snowplow driver this past winter, was another reminder of the check she'd need to write the condo association for repairs. Every spring, all over the peninsula, yards and driveways were rearranged by plows, if not consumed by mud season. Thank goodness she had the funds and wouldn't have to serve up her expensive and much-loved pearls for any reason.

In the background, the table gleamed even more than it had when she'd put it all together earlier in the morning.

The sun had found its way in through the large window, and it now touched the newly polished cutlery and heirloom crystal, sending small whorls of light bouncing off the nearby wall. Matching curlicues from the etched glass of two hurricanes joined the wall art and highlighted the thick blue pillar candles she had just thought to light.

Hazel was a list maker and had left nothing to chance. Ellis was bringing Marilyn and Janet was coming on her own with a bag full of photos of Ellis from infancy onward, and a practical pie carrier to protect her prized lemon-cream, light-as-air concoction. The rest of the car seemed perpetually filled with junk moved between thrift stores and the dump.

Beyond the pretty picture window, the tide had begun its expected performance and voluminous plumes of water were targeting the rocks only to disperse into a rainbow of spray. Each time the water receded, it left behind what little sand there was giggling with foam. To think she'd almost put money down on a second-floor condominium on the east side with nothing but a miniscule view of the inner harbor!

Suddenly, with everything checked and rechecked, Hazel wrestled with the idea that she'd gone to an awful lot of trouble for a woman who so far seemed incapable of meriting such attention. Then she reminded herself that all the effort would be worth it if it helped Ellis in any way.

Even the most expensive Prosecco had been taken from Berman's Provisions, which Hazel felt would give both her daughter and granddaughter some bragging rights about the fine wines they'd begun to carry. Again, according to Janet, Marilyn often had her own events catered rather than dirty her kitchen. *We'll see*, she thought as she heard a soft knock at the front door.

"Welcome," Hazel said air-kissing Marilyn's cheek. "I'm so glad this date worked out for you, and turning to her daughter and granddaughter, "and don't you both look nice and summery!"

"Even from the doorway, everything looks wonderful, Gran."

"It certainly does, Hazel, and how nice you've been able to convert such a simple unit to suit your tastes," Marilyn said.

Seeing Marilyn's pearls, Hazel shifted her eyes just enough to avoid an eruption of laughter while she cleared her throat. *So much for that.* Marilyn's hair, an arresting shade of white and worn just below the chin, looked nothing like the last time Hazel had laid eyes on her, and was perhaps the white that would consume Artie's salt and pepper shade that made the girls call him Dr. McDreamy. Hazel envied the natural luster of Marilyn's hair; her own would never attain such a glorious white. But as she ushered Marilyn into the living room, she studiously averted her eyes away from the pearls that Marilyn insisted on calling attention to with her long fingernails. "Well, Ellis played a role too; she has a wonderful eye for design."

"She was telling me on the way over about some of the things she's planning to do at Berman's as well."

"I think she gets most of her creativity from her grandfather," Hazel said.

"I don't think there's much room for creativity where they're living now, which is why I wish they'd find a proper house to settle into after the wedding. That cottage is hardly big enough to entertain."

Ouch. Hazel attempted to soften the sting, saying, "I do pretty well in that department, Marilyn, even in this little place."

"I think we'll be a little too busy for any heavy entertaining for a while," Ellis said walking toward the kitchen, "But we've had some fun gatherings there already. You'll see, we'll make it work."

"Yes, I know, but hopefully you'll get to slow down when you start a family, and then you'll want space to raise them and hold larger family gatherings."

Not ten minutes in, and everything was *turning to shit*—Midge had somehow entered the conversation; a voice from beyond that Hazel didn't need at the moment.

"We might be getting a little ahead of ourselves; after all, they haven't even walked down the aisle yet."

Janet, who'd kept her mouth shut during the exchange now said, "It isn't the same as when we got married Marilyn. These kids like to take care of their careers first nowadays."

Ellis was feeling the heat, and taking off the cardigan she'd worn only because it matched her turquoise shift, she said, "Mom, why don't you help me get out the wine, and we can put your pie in the fridge."

Hazel took her cue, and brought Marilyn to the window, which was always a wonderful talking point. "We need the Zin," Hazel called to Ellis, and then turning back to her guest, "I'm so glad I live so close to the ocean."

"Look at that spray; isn't it a pain to have to clean all this glass?"

"It's well worth the effort, believe me." Hazel kept watching Marilyn's pursed expression. "Obviously, I don't go out there and clean them myself, but the maintenance man says he doesn't consider it work with a view like this."

Worry snaked across the back of Ellis's neck. "Shall I bring the appetizers over to the cocktail table?" She was already struggling with the tension and veiled inuendo and the almost palpable dead space between thoughts, and she knew without question what words were rolling around in her grandmother's brain. But what composure, Ellis thought, to be able to ward off what could easily turn to disaster. There were lessons to be learned here.

"Yes, please," Hazel replied. "I'm sure Marilyn must be hungry by now." Hazel watched as Marilyn's chin lifted ever so slightly, or maybe it was the way she looked when she sniffed.

"I fixed a good breakfast; Artie always says I'm too thin."

"Artie's a considerate man," Janet offered.

Ellis's eyes flicked back and forth; it was a struggle to keep the ball in play, but as she walked to the living room, she jumped in to finish her mother's thought. "He's been a huge help to my parents."

"That's why I don't want him to burn himself out with working two jobs," Marilyn said.

"He told me he loves working with Linden."

"Mom, we have to look at her point of view too," Ellis said as she set the tray down on the low table. "Good thing you don't have to watch your weight, Marilyn. These little cheese puffs are to die for."

Before talk of waistlines could stir up trouble, Hazel took Marilyn, holding one of the puffs daintily on a napkin, through the rest of the efficient apartment. "I know Ellis is anxious to share our experience at the Colony and about all their dresses once we've finished lunch. The hotel hasn't changed much in the fifty years since my best friend was married there, and it's still a really beautiful setting for a wedding."

"Arthur and I stayed there once," Marilyn offered. "A little far away for my taste though."

Janet had also worried that the venue was too far from home, but then Artie assured everyone that their friends were all excited to be taking a 'road trip' down the coast. But, now, guessing from Marilyn's demeanor it wasn't the distance but the probability that there'd be fewer people for her to laud it over. Those who'd never experienced such a classy place. "Ellis made overnight reservations for family so it'll be quite easy for you," Hazel said.

"They seemed to have forgotten to ask my opinion."

Ah, the crux of this odd behavior, Hazel thought, circling back to the living room as Marilyn's face turned pinker than her natural complexion warranted. "Well, you know how the younger set are these days. They like doing things on their own, and those two are really not that young, are they?"

"No, but this *is* Artie's first marriage," Marilyn said.

Zinger number two, or maybe four, she'd lost count. "Ellis why don't you help me with the food while your mom shows off some of those baby pictures you kids were talking about for your display board." Hazel knew she had to go in the kitchen and set the meal in motion or something rude was going to leave her own mouth.

Ellis groaned under her breath, "Sure Gran; what can I do?"

"Fill the water glasses and dress the salad, please. The dressing is in the Mason jar on the kitchen counter."

Janet took a pile of snapshots from her carry bag and splayed them out like playing cards in front of Marilyn. "We didn't do this in our day, but I guess it's something to break the ice and have a good laugh over with all their friends."

"We didn't do that either."

"Linden and I were saying just last night how good looking they both are and if they have kids, how adorable they'll be."

"*If?* I would think children were a high priority given Ellis's age, even if she wants to work a while longer."

Hazel bit her tongue. The words carried across the short distance between the living room and kitchen, and all her grand hopes were quickly fading. She had to take control somehow—Ellis was looking speared-through. "Let's not project too far ahead; we haven't even had the pleasure of the wedding yet." Hazel looked across at Janet, who'd just abruptly stood up; a frown was now plastered on her flushed face.

"I feel a hot flash coming on, Mom; I'm going to duck outside for a minute."

That's my girl. Hazel's hope rose up with the red of Janet's neck; her daughter wasn't going to let this new foe get the best of her, not before lunch at least. "Marilyn, how about you give us a hand here; we're family after all."

Marilyn smoothed down the front of her patterned dress, "Do you have an apron?"

"No problem, but there isn't any extra juice on the platter." Hazel turned to get an apron out of the drawer, but Marilyn had already moved. "While you get that to the table, I'll slice the bread, and Ellis, you put the cheese puffs back in the fridge."

"Will do." Ellis raised her voice toward Marilyn. "I brought the photos of my wedding dress to look at after lunch. What with the new date, I ended up buying online, and even though he won't see it until the big day, I think Artie would like knowing you were part of this."

"It would have been nice if he'd mentioned any of that to me, but he's becoming more and more like his father who was always just as parsimonious."

What the hell, thought Hazel—*parsimonious*? What provokes her to talk like that? Artie would probably rather not say anything than incur such trite drivel. "Oh, there you are Janet, just in time."

"Those things don't last long, but what a pain in the ass they are."

"Mom, you sit over here." Ellis was grateful for the oval-shaped table and instinctively chose a chair on the end. And, moving to the opposite end, she said, "You're here Marilyn."

"You set a pretty table, Hazel," Marilyn said.

"I don't know if it's just my generation, but I've always enjoyed entertaining."

"I used to do quite a lot of it, but the harbor has changed a lot for me since Arthur died."

"Really, in what way?"

"My mahjong gang has broken up, the bridge group disbanded, and no one ever wants to have cocktails anymore. They've always got an excuse not to get together. It's quite maddening."

More like everyone jumped ship, thought Hazel. "That's too bad, but I'm sure you'll make new friends over the summer."

"Maybe so, but I'm not holding out much hope. There seems to be a new breed of summer people at every function I attend. It's just not the same anymore."

Earth to Marilyn! Hazel picked up a fork and took a deep breath, "Let's dig in before the chicken gets cold, shall we?"

Hazel's indignation swelled silently as she tried to digest not only her food, which she'd hardly tasted, but Marilyn's one-of-a-kind nature. The meal itself was delicious as always when she put in the effort, but Hazel's stomach was beginning to rebel. She surveyed the table, noting the bread being passed, the wine bottle emptying, and the knives and forks barely tapping the delicate porcelain. All the while, keeping a neutral expression, as did Janet, who chewed thoughtfully and occasionally waved her little topper away from her chest. Marilyn was the only one who was about to clean her plate, and Ellis looked on the verge of tears. In that moment, Hazel realized how tough it might be for her granddaughter to hold her own against the arrogant woman who was about to officially become family. This, Hazel thought, was far tougher than she'd imagined, and for once, Janet wasn't just spewing gossip. That woman might be the real deal—the-mother-in-law from hell.

"Anyone ready for pie?"

Hazel watched Janet's rigid posture as she walked away from the table. "The plates are right there on the counter, dear." Other than Marilyn, the main course had only been trifled with, but Hazel knew her daughter was about to lose it. "We'll have it in the living room, Janet, where the light's better, and in the meantime, I'll get the coffee cups from the hutch." Hazel said and then cursed herself for deciding to go all out. "And while you're in the fridge, take out the new Prosecco please."

Marilyn hadn't waited to be asked, but had come to the counter with her empty plate, the bread basket and her glass, and Hazel tried another tack. "This is nice, Marilyn; I hope there'll be many more such get-togethers."

"Artie said you were a good cook, and he was right. I don't think he's as fussy an eater as he was, but it's hard to tell these days."

"I used to entertain quite often. But like you said, things change when we're widowed."

Hazel watched as her guest considered the comment. *She's lonely and that's sad.* "You and Janet will have your hands full when the kids are married and you're hosting dinners back and forth."

Janet jumped in before her mother could assign dates to those so-called get-togethers, "I'm more of a baker than a chef," she said. "But you can always count on me for dessert."

Hazel sprang into action--a small 'o' had formed on Marilyn's lips, a precursor to what would probably be another snipe aimed this time at Janet's newly rounded out figure. "You'll get to sample the pie that won a blue ribbon in just a few minutes," Hazel said. "Go join Ellis and make yourself comfortable while we bring everything over."

"If you'll excuse me, I'll use your powder room first."

"Mom," Janet whispered once Marilyn was out of earshot, "What the hell are you doing, offering me up like that?"

"Don't worry, she won't take you up on it. She's lonely and maybe a little extra kindness will help break apart that brittle shell she's wearing."

"A sledge hammer couldn't do that."

"Now Janet, please. I admit you were right, but we have to stand together for Ellis's sake."

"Maybe you'd like to come with us for the next fitting," Ellis said once they'd all settled in the living room. "Gran's the only one whose seen it in person and she thinks this slim-line, off-the shoulder is flattering."

"My opinion doesn't count as much; she knows I'd love her in anything," Janet said.

"Is it supposed to be so white, or is that just the way it's printed?" Marilyn asked.

Ellis thought she was having one of her mother's hot flashes. "Why?"

"It's just that with your skin tone, you'd look lovely in a cream or ivory shade, don't you think, Janet?"

Hazel watched the daggers, helpless in what was turning into a power struggle as Janet said, "If you're implying white is a symbol of virginity, Marilyn, most couples are living together these days, so it's a bit ridiculous to expect them all to go without a white wedding." Hazel watched as Marilyn shifted in her seat. "I have a friend whose daughter is also divorced, that's all I was thinking of, and she opted for an off-tone and *she* looked positively stunning."

Did she hear hissing in the room, Hazel wondered? She looked at Janet who looked poised to pounce, but forced herself to step in before their words escalated. "I think we're getting off on the wrong foot here."

Ignoring Hazel, Ellis turned to Marilyn and said, "I was hoping to surprise you, not upset you."

"I guess since you're not being married in a church it really doesn't matter what I think about your dress color."

"Is that what's bothering you, that I don't follow any particular religion?"

"Well even though Artie's become a *lapsed* Catholic, it would have been nice to follow our family's traditions."

"Neither of us wanted a religious ceremony, Marilyn. I hope you can respect that."

"What choice do I have? Perhaps that's why neither of you are paying attention to what will happen to the souls of your future children if they're not given the basics."

Ellis stood up and said, "Does Artie know how you feel about this?"

"Of course, he does!"

"This is the first time I'm hearing anything about it."

Ellis felt her heart racing; what else might he be keeping from her.

"Maybe this isn't the time to be discussing this, Marilyn. It's obvious there are issues they're going to have to deal with in private, and I don't think it's our place to be meddling, especially since our family has never been steeped in religious beliefs. And that doesn't have anything to do with the mis-steps of the Catholic Church these days," Hazel said.

Janet was now also on her feet, "This is plain nonsense, Marilyn. Which is it—her divorce or her religion? Or is it something else you're finding fault with?"

"Well I don't' understand why everyone's so upset; I didn't say anything that wasn't fact," Marilyn shot back.

"No, you didn't. But it implies you might think I'm unsuitable to be your daughter-in-law."

"Ohfortheloveofgod…you are all way over-sensitive. I only meant that…"

"We know what you meant, Marilyn," said Hazel. "We certainly wouldn't want Artie to get the impression you're unhappy with his choice, now would we?"

"He's the one I'm thinking about; we've never had a divorce in our family and my Artie would be destroyed if it happened."

"Do you know something we don't?" asked Hazel before Janet had a chance.

"Well look how she walked out on that fine young lawyer?"

Now we're getting somewhere, thought Hazel. "If you knew the real circumstances, I think you'd be a little kinder about this. And for the record, Artie does know all the details. And, it's really none of anyone else's business is it?"

"Does it matter? It's just not how I'd hoped, that's all."

"Damn it, Marilyn, do you realize how you sound?" Hazel almost had to bite her tongue to keep from saying more.

"I know how it sounds, Gran, but apparently Marilyn really doesn't think I'm good enough for her precious son."

"I'm sorry Mom, but I have something important to do at home," Janet said. "I'll be back tomorrow to pick up my things. You're still welcome to come with us for Ellis's fitting, Marilyn, because it's the right thing to do. But I have to ask you to respect her wishes...understand?"

Hazel got up, leaving Marilyn open-mouthed, and Ellis headed for the bathroom while Hazel walked Janet to the door. "Bravo, but please let this be the last outburst."

"Told you, right?"

"Yes dear, and you were right. But it's our girl's heart at stake here and neither of us wants it broken. We'll find our way."

Hazel walked back into the living room just as Ellis appeared from the hall bathroom. Small tendrils of hair framing her face appeared damp and messier than when she'd first arrived. Marilyn was just sitting there staring out to sea. "Coffee, anyone?" Hazel said.

"Okay, okay, I stand corrected," Marilyn said at last. "I wish Janet hadn't left, but you have to know, he's all I have left here. Sheila hardly ever visits, so I don't get to see my grandbabies, who by the way, were baptized in the Church so I didn't think it would be an issue for Artie. And now I feel like I'm losing him."

"What's that old saying, Marilyn, about not losing a son, but gaining a daughter?" Hazel said. "Maybe it's time you focus on that."

Ellis moved over and put an arm around Marilyn's shoulder. "It's up to you, but I'd really like you to be part of all of this," she said pointing to the wedding dress. "And just so you know, I'm not telling Artie what you said—not this time anyway."

Hazel could tell by the set of her face, that Marilyn was trying hard not to cry. "Can I give you a piece of pie to go?"

"I'd like that, and I'll call Janet tomorrow. I have some ass-kissing to do."

Hazel opened her eyes wide, "I believe you do Marilyn; I believe you do."

194

~

"Holy hell, Gran. What just happened?"

"I think someone had a come-to-Jesus moment, and I couldn't be happier." Hazel was even happier that Marilyn was now out in the car. "Let's just hope she doesn't backslide."

"Mothers-in-law are notorious for being difficult, right? I mean it's not just because of me?"

For all this new-age know-how, her granddaughter didn't have a clue about women like Marilyn. "Sweetheart, it most certainly is not because of you. She's lonely, that's all. Sometimes a husband, even one you don't always agree with, can be a buffer for situations like this. I dare say if Arthur were still alive, she'd be talking a different tune. Now you go along before she decides to come back in after you."

"I'm whipped and it's only four-thirty. Can I take some leftovers to have for our dinner tonight, otherwise, I'm afraid I'll be opening cans?" Ellis said. "I know I promised I wouldn't tell Artie, but what do I say when he asks, and I know he will."

"Tell him the truth—that she's going to go along for your next fitting. And that maybe the two of you should invite her over for a meal in the very near future."

"How come you're so smart?"

"It's a Beane thing."

"You say that all the time. Why?"

"Habit…it's what Midge always said, and it's a damn sight easier than coming up with answers on the fly. Now let's get you boxed up; there's more than enough for you to take home."

As soon as Ellis left, Hazel gave in to the chill left behind by Marilyn's poor manners by switching on the fireplace for its warming ambiance and turning up the volume on a favorite piece of music to make herself feel better. She went into the kitchen and filled the dishwasher and took the table linens into the laundry alcove. And then, as if it would clear away the bad taste in her mouth, she poured herself another glass of Prosecco. It made her happy to know that she'd be able to hear the instruments pleading to her from wherever she was in the condo, and especially with a tough day finally at her back. Once she was finished cleaning up, she went in and sat in front of the fire and put her feet up. Her head was bursting with wedding chatter, all that nonsense about shades of white, which made her summon up her own wedding dress—simple and white, even with everything she'd put herself through. They'd had a small ceremony, which had thrown Mother Mowry for a loop since she certainly had no clue about anything. Their reception had been held at The Village Inn, which oddly, was now the site of the local post office. Their menu, like just about every restaurant, had featured what was so popularly referred to in those days as rubber chicken. For everyone's sake, Hazel hoped that the menu she'd talked Ellis into wouldn't involve anything remotely overcooked or gray and disguised with a brown sauce, or Hazel thought, they would all be hearing about it forever. Just like Ellis's gown, which might pass muster now, but wait until Ellis decided to cut it up and rearrange it into a street-length party dress, white as a sheet, which then might slap old Marilyn right in the face of her hardboiled ideas.

Oh, the day had definitely gotten to her, Hazel realized and then remembered that even Sloane had hung onto her snow-white gown hoping to be able to reinvent it for another use one day. Unfortunately, like so many bridal dresses, it was put away until it was thrown away for turning gray with age.

But there would always be issues with someone like Marilyn; if not the gown, it might be Ellis's cooking or housekeeping habits. Or Artie might show up at Marilyn's house dressed for dinner only to find she blames Ellis for his choice in clothes. A woman like Marilyn would be discontented with whatever might be tossed in her lap.

Hazel looked over at the family photo taken out on Monhegan, recognizing how Ellis was just beginning to come into her own at that juncture, and with no idea of her inherited strengths, the survival instinct she would soon learn to lean on because of women like Midge and those before her. Then, as her sleepy gaze fell on the old Bible, Hazel was reminded of the women listed in there who'd grown tough of necessity, their hardscrabble lives a testament to the blood running through her granddaughter's veins.

In this twenty-first century, those Maine women might be wildly out of fashion, but they were the keenest reminder of how far removed Ellis and her peers were from a life of duty over happiness.

Before calling it a night, Hazel went over to the bookcase and took down the hefty Bible without removing it from the sealed bag. It was in dire need of rebinding, but Hazel was now certain that Ellis should have it before it fell apart or before something happened; Hazel was no spring chicken after all. She made a mental note to list it among the belongings already in the codicil of her updated will. Sadly, Janet had no interest in delving into the past. *My girl, my girl,* Hazel thought as she pressed the wrapped Bible to her chest. Where would her daughter align herself as she aged, what power would she choose to herald in her later years when she needed the comfort of connection over useless chatter.

You're definitely feeling your age tonight. Hazel often mused this way, but tonight her thoughts were taking her to places she was almost too tired to go. She would provide assistance as best she could, but for all her concerns, Janet was a wonderful mother, even if she was not always as centered as Hazel would have liked, especially since the onset of menopause. But Janet would do a bang-up job helping with a wedding shower if that was a direction in which she wanted to go, and would lavish the bridesmaids with attention and kindness. And, Linden would be there for Artie and his band of heartthrobs. Hazel's tired brain slipped back to how it had been during Sloane's events, the tittering and flirting and oh-so-much hair teasing and make-up experimenting. Things weren't awfully different now, except that as far as Hazel knew, no one was hiding any big secret.

As she pushed through a mental calendar, she thought about the upcoming trip to Portland for that final fitting and worried whether or not she had the energy for another possible go-round with Marilyn. Feeling her eyelids drooping, Hazel switched everything off and stared at the quarter moon. Dreams would come if they must, but she wasn't going to encourage them. The day had done her in.

Chapter 18

After long and sometimes brutal winters, it's always a surprise when coastal towns come alive for the season in what looks like an overnight process instead of weeks of cleanup and organization and restocking of shelves. Boothbay Harbor was one of those towns; people stream in from away, parking meters go up, flags are set out and barrels and urns are filled with flowers in front of the many stores and restaurants. Maine is open for business.

Canons boom as historic schooners sail into the harbor on Windjammers' Day, parades and music mark the week, and love is in the air. On decks and docks and backyards and boats and once in a while on Fisherman's Island. June is a notoriously popular month for weddings, but this summer the calendar in Hazel's kitchen matched the one in her daughter's as well as her granddaughter's, each ticking off the number of days racing toward August and Ellis and Artie's chance to claim their space on the wedding docket.

Soon the trivial would be turned into tantamount. The weeks flew by: fittings, accessories, hairstyles, and music were all being debated. As well as whether or not it was appropriate for the bride to wear sneakers with her gown for dancing. And everyone watched the weather. Humidity had set in and the California contingent were due to arrive just in time to party. Toasts to the boys in blue were handled through Skype until such time as they could do so in person, and gifts arrived daily for the future Mrs. Granger. The wedding was only three weeks away.

~

"What's that banging?" Ellis asked. She was glad to have him out from underfoot for a while. They'd had the *talk* about Marilyn, hours and hours of talking that led to Ellis dissolving in tears and Artie helpless to try and figure out how to resolve the situation. And every day since she had tried to hold her tongue.

Artie stuck his phone out of the truck window so she'd hear what the racket really sounded like. "Coming from Commercial Street, another damn rehab."

"Don't go getting all cross; there's nothing you can do about it," Ellis said. "Do you think we should invite Mrs. Johnson from across the street?"

"You can't keep changing the numbers," Artie said. "There's a cut-off date, and besides we can't invite everyone who's been kind enough to send a congratulatory card. Your family's well known, but we can't have Hazel thinking we're milking a good thing."

"Fine, I'll just have to feel bad whenever I see her."

"A little dramatic, don't you think, and besides haven't they all gone out?"

"I have a few left so I was going to hand deliver it."

"Do what you need to, I'm not going to argue over it now. There's enough on my plate today." He really didn't have *so* much going on, but his mood had turned sour and if he stopped in to see Linden, which had been his intention, they'd both be gnawing on the same bone: the grandiose way Linden's beloved town was changing. He considered it *his* town more than Artie had, since he'd at one time nursed the idea of going out west with his other two best friends. But Boothbay Harbor was home now and he'd made peace with the fact that it always would be.

"Don't forget to check and see if they carry those labels we talked about."

"There's a line of people waiting to get in."

"Uh oh, I forgot this is a book-signing Saturday, sorry."

"Don't worry, I'm doing a head count of the tourists in town this morning."

"That many, huh?"

"I stopped by Hannaford's on my way here—the shopping carts have sprouted up all over the parking lot like radical plants—'cause no one puts them back!

"This happens to you every summer and every

summer you go a little bit nutty."

"The line's moving, gotta run." Artie knew how annoyed Ellis got whenever he bitched about all those PFAs but he just couldn't help himself. He wasn't the typical poster boy for the Chamber of Commerce and that was fine by him. They put the fire in the belly of vacationers, luring them to the water's edge and tops of mountain ranges—and gladly watched the fire go out right after Labor Day, or at least by the time the summer water was turned off in October. It was the same revolving door that seasonal places everywhere endured because that was just the way it was if you wanted to earn a living. He'll probably bitch about the dead of winter too; that also came with the territory.

Hometowns could be the best and the worst for families who'd lived in them forever. They'd seen it all, been rankled by much, and could usually change very little. The Corbishleys were on the same list as the Mowrys and Bermans, but not the Grangers since Artie's mother had been force-fed Maine by the very amiable Arthur Granger. And, sadly, Artie thought as he got out of the truck, his mother rarely let him forget where she came from. And she wasn't letting up on any of her harping either even though the wedding date was right around the corner. And he didn't know how to combat any of it. And on top of that, Ellis had been leaving sticky notes around their cottage as a constant reminder, and today, she'd planted one on the brim of his cap: choose the music; check in with the Notary. And now, it was labels. How did women keep track of so much, he wondered as he spotted a few more kayak-topped cars adding even more color to the streets already filled with shoppers and a team of neon-Lycra dressed cyclists trying to make their way through the crowd. With all the activity, the echo of a lose stay against a mast was barely audible but he pretty much knew it was Johnny Bale's boat, as always, when he moored her carelessly. The guy couldn't handle his drink, Artie thought as he walked into the bookstore. He immediately spotted Chad's head above a cluster of women at the register. Artie watched the way his best friend schmoozed them all, no matter their ages. As a highly eligible bachelor, he was totally in his element, and Artie had a sneaking feeling Chad thought of himself a little like the reality TV bachelors, and in truth, he was good looking enough to be one. Ellis constantly reminded him that Chad dressed better than most of the local guys too. No ball caps and plaid shirts for him, just those expensive polos like the golfers wore and chinos and brand-name boat shoes all summer long, and yet he could talk fishing down at the docks with the best of them.

Artie looked down at what he'd thrown on that morning: tee shirt, cargo shorts and work boots with ratty socks peeking over the tops. He might not dress like Chad, but he could keep up with the fishing. They'd caught a record number of stripers together, but as close as they were, they were as different as they could be when it came to women. And today, Chad was certainly getting plenty of attention. Artie strode over to the counter and said, "Hey old man, got any good books for sale?"

"Look who's talking" Chad said. "Come to see if I work as hard as you claim to? Or, is it because you're putty in Ellis's hands?"

"Jealous, huh? Of course, I can't blame you; how long's it been since you've had such good luck?"

"That's a dangerous question my friend, and unfit for disclosure without the proper setting…say a quick beer at Brown's before you go home?"

"That'll work, but I'm here on a mission, strictly wedding related."

"Come in back, I've been listening to those sound tracks you forwarded."

"I owe you buddy, and I mean big time!"

"And I will collect! So, tell me, how're the rest of the wedding details coming along? Anything I should know about that I don't already?"

"Just that if we don't decide on which band, my ass is cooked."

"Look, bud, you have two choices only and let me just

say this…if you go with the big band sound, your girl's going to expect you to dance to everything. If you choose the jazz band, no one's really going to be able to do a lot of dancing even if we'll have some great listening music while we drink the night away."

"I'm screwed, right?"

"How about we figure out how you can wing it on the dance floor and we go for the big band."

Before Artie could reply, a really cute, dark-haired girl who looked to be in her mid-twenties rushed forward, managing to nudge Artie out of the way. He winked at Chad, "Catch you later Romeo."

"Say three at Brown's?"

Artie gave him a thumbs up as he turned away, but he knew without question, that Chad would be trying to hold her attention while simultaneously flipping the bird at Artie behind her back.

Chapter 19

Ellis finished up her gardening and returned to the kitchen where she found a post-it-note from Artie stuck to the coffee pot. "Big tease," Ellis said, ripping the little pink square off the pot and tossing it into the trash. She removed her soiled gloves and got an ice cube from the freezer and added it to her empty cup and then filled it with the now lukewarm coffee. If she hadn't had other more important things to do with her morning, she might have been tempted to concoct a few infuriating jokes to retaliate, but she had to make a stop at her grandmother's and then a quick stop at Jeanie's to show her the table decorations that had just arrived. Getting back at Artie would just have to wait until later.

Once she'd showered and changed into a tank top and shorts, she rang her grandmother's number only to be met with a disembodied voice on the other end. Ellis had her own key, and Gran had always given her carte-blanche about using it. Ellis hadn't said anything due to her grandmother's ego—she'd refused to even consider wearing one of those life-alert buttons—but having the spare key might turn out to be a lifesaver down the road.

Getting into her cherished but old blue Honda Civic, Ellis thought of how much her grandmother had done for her already, not the least of which was finding the perfect dress for Ellis's mother to wear for the wedding. And, thanks to Gran's irrepressible energy and love for the mighty Mall, Janet now had a lovely theme-related dress that would hide not only her mid-section, but was the right material to help combat those awful hot flashes, which she declared would never go away, ever! Hail the Mowry women, her mother had declared, even though technically Ellis was not. After her divorce, she'd given a great deal of thought to adopting the Mowry name formally instead of going back to Berman, to avoid anything that might have continued to connect her to Walter, but that had all become a moot point once she knew she was to become a Granger. And, unlike her ex, Artie had never made her feel the way Walter had—that she was no more than a proving ground for his manhood. She shuddered to think of those wasted years. And then she realized she'd driven halfway to her grandmother's without paying attention to the winding, lazy turns on the roads heading east and had sped right past the East Boothbay General Store where she had intended to grab a container of salad-to-go. She was about a mile from Ocean Point when she rolled down the car windows. She sneezed—once, twice, and on the third she thought of her future mother-in-law and her prohibition on pets in the home. *Screw that.* By the time the season changed and another form of allergen was out there, she'd be the new Mrs. Granger and, who knew, maybe even adopt a cat.

As she took the final turn onto her grandmother's road, the air changed again, and the smell of salt was strong enough to taste. She felt invigorated and amazingly slim since she'd cut out non-essential carbs. And, in spite of Marilyn's previous and not-so-coy hints, Ellis knew Artie was more than ready to become her husband.

Pulling into the parking space designated for visitors, Ellis checked her watch. It was just shy of eleven; she had plenty of time to steal a final peek at the family Bible. She'd finally remembered that her grandmother had a standing appointment with her hairdresser and then lunch with her friend Millie. Ellis let herself into the condo and dropped her keys on the entry stand. The space was neat and picture perfect as always, and the view just as drop-dead gorgeous and very much like entering an oasis—soft appealing colors, wide windows unfettered by curtains, and a cloudless expanse of blue sky beyond. Her grandmother had a good eye, Ellis thought as she went through to the kitchen. Gran always kept a pitcher of fresh squeezed orange juice in the fridge.

Ellis filled a glass and brought it into the living room and set in on a coaster. Then, she went straight to the bookshelf and removed the deteriorating Bible from a large Ziplock bag all the while holding her breath against the musty smell of old paper. She hadn't noticed the bulky wedding album on the floor next to her grandmother's desk until her foot bumped against it. She stumbled, and the infamous photo of Great-grandmother Olive H fell out of the Bible, landing face up on the desk so that her flinty eyes could demand their due.

Already this project was worse than a jigsaw puzzle with missing pieces, but in this case, there were too many Olive's in one tree. The whole gift idea was becoming almost comical. Ellis would not even entertain the idea of an Olive Granger somewhere down the line, but as she continued running through the names she'd missed on the previous go-round, she had to admit, the name Oliver had a certain pluck about it. She made a mental note to get Artie's opinion.

Instead of copying the names by hand as she had the first time, she took out her phone and snapped the remaining names written in a cursive script by Eleanor, daughter of Olive H. This was turning out to be a much larger project than she'd anticipated—connecting the dots between her family and the supposed relatives buried alongside them in the Westport Island cemetery as well as those up-country as Gran always referred to Somerset County. Ellis also had to take into consideration the number of babies that hadn't lived, adding to the many similarities in first names.

When Hazel broached the subject while they'd been at the Colony, Ellis thought she'd been caught out, but fortunately her grandmother's nod to the cemeteries had just been pure coincidence. But there was still so much to do in order to verify where the dead and buried had hailed from; as with all the Olives, there were an abundance of Davids, and only some of them identified by a different middle name or initial. As the trail went further back in time, there were duplicate Johns and Timothys and Thomases—faceless names associated with skimpy facts, so that even with cross-referencing their spouses and children, the search often led to an inconclusive match. She would be spending a lot more time verifying before she could affix them to their rightful place on the family tree.

When she finished photographing the entire record, she put her phone in her pocket and slid the Bible back inside the Ziplock and tucked it between the mystery novels her grandmother devoured.

When Ellis turned around, the sea had flattened, and large patches of water looked as if it had been splatter-painted by a wildly enthusiastic artist. A day to celebrate, she thought as she remembered the small amount of a stoppered Prosecco still left in the fridge, a wonderful way to enhance her remaining juice.

A clear outline of Monhegan Island sat on the horizon, an unspoiled rock not ten miles from home and the perfect place for a honeymoon. Time to voice their blessings and let the wind carry their words across the sea. A magical place that no matter how many times they'd been, would never be enough. Five full days with nothing to do but explore both the scenery and each other as a married couple. She scanned the living room for photos her grandfather had taken of the family on Monhegan.

In place of plants, the few photographs displayed were clumped on an antique plant stand: a picture of Jake in uniform, his toothy grin so like their father's; one of the Squirrel Islanders as they exited the *Nellie G*, which must have been the day Gran and Millie went sea glass hunting; and, there in a rustic frame, a group photo from Monhegan, which she knew had been taken by some willing passerby.

Ellis kissed the tip of her finger and placed it on the glass right above her grandfather's head. *Not enough time with you, not by a longshot.*

Her grandmother had winnowed down the plants she'd kept alive in the big house on the hill, and brought her favorites here, mostly because Ellis's mother would have forgotten to water them. The mature ferns now had a place of honor near the sunniest window. They'd grown overly large in her grandmother's care and all but obscured a bright-patterned ottoman, which had been a gift her grandfather had shipped home from one of their foreign destinations in order to please his wife. Ellis also knew they'd been really good together, and yet, didn't Gran deserve to be happy again.

A familiar chime sounded from across the room—noon. Gran and Millie were probably on Southport ordering lobster rolls over at Robinson's at this very moment, and hopefully, they'd be chatting about the story of dancing at the Colony, since it had to still be fresh on her grandmother's mind. It would make it much easier for Ellis to entice Millie into action if she was allowed to know a little about the circumstances ahead of time. If not for Fred, the two women would spend the best days of summer eating there. Millie had framed photos of the eagles she'd photographed there as they'd swooped in and annoyed an offending gull or two while they tried to steal scraps of leftover food. Tourists often forgot that gulls were terrible bandits. Ellis, who'd had a good teacher, had always been fascinated by gull behavior, especially their concentration as they hovered low over returning lobster boats, their long wings folded in a way that created a cluster of origami figures. She'd never actually seen them steal a lobster off a boat, but maybe her grandfather had just told her that to keep her satisfied. And, thinking of lobsters, she suddenly realized she was hungry. Gran would encourage her if she were here, Ellis thought. After all, the lone wedge of tomato tart was just sitting there next to the juice and would probably be dried out by the next day anyway. Mentally counting out the carbs, she wolfed down the thin-crusted tart and then went back into the living room for that long-awaited look at the album she had been told so much about. She sat down on the sofa and rested it on her knees, thinking that if nothing else, she might find something she could incorporate into her own theme with the little time left. She reckoned Eduardo would have been behind the camera so she could hardly expect to see what he looked like. And even if he had been caught by someone else's camera, would he have stood out in a crowd of New Englanders. *Yes,* she thought, back then he probably would have.

Ellis quickly realized that this album was unlike any she'd ever seen or even heard of. It was a thickly padded cover with a small cut-out for the formal bridal picture. Inside, silly triangular corners were doing very little to keep the photos from falling off the pages, and she adjusted her position so nothing would fall on the floor. The pages crackled and the pictures were smudged from handling and she wondered how many times they might have been caressed in the aftermath of her grandfather's death. Ellis looked at the man she revered; it was the photo her grandmother had brought to the Colony and had not yet made it back into its designated slot. But the more she stared at his picture, the harder it was to reconcile it with the man he'd become. The thin, twenty-something had evolved over his lifetime into a solidly built and far more handsome man, becoming both charming and very successful.

Ellis smoothed her finger over the cowlick he'd never quite tamed. Maybe it was true, that men aged better than women: gray hair meant distinguished looking; wrinkles added dimension to their years of experience; it just wasn't fair at all.

And there was Gran, of course—slimmer even in the dark blue maid of honor's dress, and poised for something Ellis couldn't read on a face that was only a little like her own.

Suddenly, she was lost in a sea of classic 1960s hairdos. The older women seemed to prefer the tight perms, but the younger set had everything from bobs with bangs to voluminous headdresses made by extreme hair-teasing and ended just at the shoulder with a flirty flip. Two of the more waif-like bridesmaids had saucer-sized eyes peering out of heavily mascaraed lashes beneath fringed hairdos, reminiscent of a model popular during the Beatles era. Some of the twenty-something girls were wearing a drop-waist style dress in bright colors. *This is better than watching old movies,* she thought as she turned page after page before she realized how much she would like to find a way to memorialize her own wedding so that one day someone might look at their album with admiration and maybe a little delighted surprise.

There were three photographs taken from different angles of the cake cutting ceremony, which is the way her grandmother had worded it. These reinforced Ellis's stance about not having a cake topper, because the smallest round tier of Sloane's cake was noticeably tilting, and the miniature bride and groom dolls were an unflattering depiction of a couple who themselves could have been movie stars.

It's an obscenely large cake, Ellis thought. Artie would, with encouragement from Chad in particular, make sure he got every last crumb in her mouth. *Not gonna happen.* This little stroll through her grandmother's memories was becoming very freeing to say the least.

One page in the album was simply titled, 'Dances'. First, there was a group doing the slide, and Ellis only knew that because she'd seen it danced at a charity party put on by those of her grandmother's generation. Next was the jitterbug. Hair flying, skirts twirling, drinks sloshing (because some of the guys on the sidelines were laughing themselves silly).

Slow dancing—pretty much the same everywhere, except for the arm positions. Older crowd: extended arms with good posture and concentration. Younger crowd: arms draped over and around shoulders and waist, lazy smiles and posture, and sizzling heat. *Some things never change.* She really was having a good time going from page to page, making up her own scenarios about this couple or that man, and her grandmother hadn't said a thing about flower girls and here were two of the cutest miniature brides she'd ever seen, right down to an itty-bitty length of netting attached to their flowered wreaths. Adorable. But, also not included in Ellis's retinue of attendants.

Finally, noticing the time, she backtracked and began to trace her finger over each page all over again in search of one man who might be considered exotic, which she finally realized was harder than she'd thought because of her own homogenized view of the world.

The ballroom photo, which had been put back where it belonged, confirmed again that the space could be just as beautiful for her own wedding. The woodwork gleamed, the chandeliers sparkled with teardrops she could almost hear tinkling against one another as they lit up the parquet flooring and rich carpeting. One idea she hadn't considered before was the way Sloane had carried out her theme by using blue vases of all sizes crammed with white flowers and placed on every available surface.

The bridesmaids' bouquets under different light conditions, were in actuality, hued with pink and trailing blue ribbons, something that hadn't been clear when she'd looked at the photos while at the Colony. Maybe it had been the early morning lighting that obscured the color, but the pink was off-putting, and Ellis had already planned on using a sharper contrast to the ombre shades, but she tucked the thought away just in case.

Then, before she closed the album, she saw one impressive photograph her grandmother had not brought to the Colony: Sloane in her exquisite white silk dress. She beamed adoringly at her husband whose arm encircled her waist just beneath a white velvet stole, both providing warmth against the October chill, and one of the most romantic-looking pictures Ellis had ever seen.

She was suddenly jealous of the gown's perfection, which she knew wouldn't have made any difference to Marilyn Granger's notions of propriety, but which would have made Ellis feel like a queen. Hers was beautiful but like so many other things about their wedding—hurriedly searched for and easier on the pocketbook. *And you don't have the figure to carry that off, you twit.* Now she sounded like Gran, she realized at the same time she noticed the light from the living room window had changed and the album had been thrown into shadow.

Even though she hadn't found the man she was looking for, or had passed him over because he didn't fit her grandmother's description and probably wouldn't have been in front of the camera anyway, Ellis had managed to find at least one new idea and a better way to view her self-imposed angst.

She closed the album and put it back where she'd found it, not at all guilty for snooping, but a tiny bit for taking that last piece of the homemade tart. A thank-you note was required; it was Gran after all. Ellis opened the desk drawer, which was just as tidy as she'd expected. Her grandmother had stacked her unpaid bills in order by their due date and tucked them into a corner alongside a small batch of blank index cards wrapped in a rubber band. Ellis pulled one of the cards out and noticed that her grandmother had saved a copy of the printed luncheon menu, which was so like her. *But what's this,* Ellis thought as she pulled on the corner of what looked to be a letter in her grandmother's funny script. *Leave it be.* Ellis stepped back and then placed the letter on top of the desk, knowing full well the battle was lost; she was after all, her mother's daughter.

And within moments of reading the entire letter, Ellis felt its full weight shifting from her grandmother's shoulders to her own. She read it a second time, and the impact of the last sentence hit her even harder.

She fought to keep from screaming out at the audacity of the man. But then her better side whispered back. Thoughts swirled and she found herself back at the

Colony, a place so engrained in her grandmother's past, but which would now be entered into Ellis's future. Without intent, she began to think of the sisterhood of women who endured far more than she ever had—even with someone like Walter. And, she thought of Jeanie, loving a man who presumably would never love her back.

And the gown Ellis envied that had so effectively covered the shame Sloane must have felt. And then Ellis tried to envision the terrible emotional pain Mike must have suffered, and her heart shifted with a compassion she hadn't known she possessed.

Dancing at the Colony, a simple act at the happiest of times, had suddenly become so much more as she began to understand the anxiety her grandmother must have gone through in an era like theirs. Ellis wasn't quite as young at the time, but she had slipped into the shallow embrace of a foolhardy marriage, and like her widowed grandmother, she too had come back stronger and hopefully, wiser.

The hotel, the rush and bustle and imagined hassle, and the full-of-frills wedding that Ellis had resisted for a while, began to take on new meaning, and that made her think of the life lessons she might one day pass on to a daughter of her own. And suddenly, that didn't seem like such an obstacle.

Putting the letter back where she had found it, she wrote out a short note on the index card and propped it against the desk lamp. Then she picked up her things and locked the door behind her. The usually refreshing chill off the water hit her full on. She took a deep breath of salty air before getting in the car. Jeanie's was the next stop, not to share what she'd found, but to come back to reality. There was no reason to bring any of this up to anyone, not even Gran.

Ellis kept her mind focused on the road, anything in order to avoid replaying the tragic circumstances, which she could hardly ever forget. And fortunately, she didn't have far to go. Jeanie lived above a garage in an apartment near West Harbor Pond that was both overheated and charming in equal measure. Ellis got out of the car and checked her messages. Artie was with Chad and was going to be late. She grabbed her big canvas tote and rushed up the stairs just as Jeanie opened the door.

"You okay?"

"Yes and no, but if you don't mind, I don't want to talk about it and it has nothing to do with the wedding."

"I ran into Chad last night."

"And?"

"And, he was hitting on some girl at least ten years younger."

"And?"

"And, I'm tired of him never noticing me."

"Do you remember that old movie, *He's Just Not That Into You?*"

"Yeah."

"Maybe it's time to start looking elsewhere?"

"I guess, but it's not that simple."

"Nothing ever is; you'd think I was pregnant the way we're scrambling with this wedding. And speaking of, how did the twins' fittings go?"

"Cindy looked terrific, but Chloe had a mini-meltdown. She'd hoped to have had the baby by the original wedding date, but now she's caught with a baby bump that made her cry because the dress looks so much better on her sister."

Oh, lord, that's all we need, a temperamental bridesmaid, which is supposed to be my department, thank you very much," Ellis said. "And, by the way, Mark is gay."

"Cindy's gonna freak; she's been talking non-stop about rekindling a high school fling."

"He obviously didn't feel the same because according to Artie who found out from Chad, Mark came out as soon as he landed in California, and apparently that bit of news never made it back here. He and his partner will be spending some time with Mark's relatives so they can join in on their annual Cabbage Island clambake."

"And Jim?"

"I guess he's still single, at least Artie hasn't said differently."

"But you're not actually rehearsing, so, what's the point of a rehearsal dinner."

"Tradition—according to both my mother and Gran. And it's not even the night before the wedding like they're supposed to be, and we still don't know where it will take place, but Artie's determined to pay for it so his mother won't be holding that over us."

"Mrs. Granger giving you a bit of agita?"

"That's an understatement, and I know he's keeping something else from me, but wherever we have it, I know it'll be a fun party and give us all a chance to catch up before we get down to the serious business of dancing at the Colony."

"I'd better alert Cindy."

"There will be other single men there and rest assured, both of you will have dance partners and who knows, maybe one of you will catch the bouquet."

Jeanie frowned. "Did you bring the centerpiece stuff?"

"See what you think." Ellis hauled out one of the big clamshell dishes that had only just arrived. "Once these are filled with either sea glass or even floating candles, I think they'll be perfect."

"I like."

"And, I brought one of the newest Chardonnays." Ellis hadn't known when she put it in the car, how much it would be needed. "Who's going to take Chloe's mind off her dress?"

"That would be the very creative Mrs. Muller and her trusty needle."

Ellis pushed aside the remaining dishes and pulled out the wine. "Let's uncork this and you can tell me what's happening at work."

"Are you sure you wouldn't like to put me on the payroll as your overseas wine scout?"

"Dr. Doolittle would miss your expert services."

"Dr. DAYLITAL wouldn't have any trouble finding another hygienist; he's a super boss."

"Pour the wine, and then we can discuss the attributes of the town's favorite dentist." Ellis would have discussed the benefits of a root canal as long as nothing else came along to shock her senseless.

"So, tell me fair friend, what other men do you have on my bucket list since you've obviously crossed Chad off for me."

"Let's see—there's Tony over at The Thistle. I hear he's newly single. Of course, you could reclaim Jeff's affection if you put a little effort into it."

"It took me half a year to untangle that relationship; why would I want to tangle it all up again."

"Might not be so bad now that she's left town."

"Jenna's still got her hooks in there somewhere and I don't trust either of them."

"I'm out of names, so you're on your own."

"You gave up too easy."

"I don't know what you're talking about; do you have any cheese to go with this wine?" Ellis couldn't tell her that she'd been feeding Chad little tidbits about the other men to make him jealous. If it worked, Jeanie would be over the moon, and if it didn't, no harm done.

"I only have crackers, no cheese."

"That's okay, I'll pass."

"That carb thing, right?"

"It worked, so yes, that carb thing, and now I'd better get my butt home and take care of what's for dinner or I will devour those crackers." Ellis wasn't even hungry, but the wine soured her stomach, or perhaps it had been the letter. "I'll check in with you tomorrow; enjoy the rest of the Chardonnay."

"You sure you're okay," Jeanie asked as she walked Ellis to the door.

"I'm fine; it's just been a big day." Then, seeing Jeanie's frown, Ellis said, I'll call you tomorrow." She waved as she got in the car and watched Jeanie go back inside before driving away. They were the best of friends and yet Ellis knew it wouldn't be right to share her grandmother's story. Ellis smiled. It might be one of those tales best served up on a deck somewhere when they too reached their seventies.

~

Artie walked through the kitchen door and saw Ellis slumped in the lawn chair on the back deck. "Hey hon, you look all pooped…too much gardening."

"I just got back from Jeanie's, but it has been quite a day."

"Want to talk about it?"

"Later maybe; right now, I just need to process a few things."

"Are you still marrying me?"

"You dope!"

'Well, I don't know how to read an ambiguous statement like that?"

"It has to do with my grandmother, not you, I promise."

"Fine, should I start up the grill?"

"Good idea, and I think I'll go have a shower and see if I can wash away some of that ambiguity."

Chapter 20

Inside the condo, Hazel sniffed the air and then followed the trail of Ellis's lily-scented moisturizer, laughing out loud even before opening the refrigerator. She walked back to the living room and noticed the album had been moved and laughed again at the mannerly thank you note. Her curious granddaughter had been rummaging again, but Hazel had opened that door when she'd told her about Sloane, so it followed that Ellis would want to see more of the wedding photos. But then, Hazel remembered where the index cards had been kept and quickly opened the desk drawer. She sighed, one of those woe-begone breaths that used to fill the empty spaces of her old house. It had been such a lovely day out with Millie. And now. Ellis would know everything, and on top of the gruesomeness outlined in the letter, how would she feel about her grandmother's indiscretion, and did any of that matter after all these years. *What's done is done.* At first, she considered whether or not to call her, and then she looked across the room to the sea beyond, and felt a sense of gratitude. Ellis always felt very at home here, and had not resented Hazel's walking away from the house John had lovingly cared for. She'd never been able to tell anyone, not even Millie, that she'd needed a change of air—the family home had been crushing her with memories and John's presence would always be as much a part of the house as the solid wood that framed it. But now, here she was five years later and thinking not so much about the man she had married, but the man who had left behind embers of hope that had cooled, but never truly been extinguished. *If she hadn't gone with Ellis, would she even be feeling all of this now?* She couldn't say that to her granddaughter either, knowing how hurtful those words would sound. Looking around at the well-appointed space—her new life—Hazel thought of the tightrope walk she was undertaking and then she took the sage from her desk drawer. What purpose had rekindling those amazing few weeks done for her. She was still alone, just daydreaming more. And at her age, she thought as she was about to light the match, dreams like that might prove hazardous to her health. She breathed in the first whiff of the pot-like aroma, which was strong and suddenly made her laugh—she still hadn't mastered the dance.

Chapter 21

Ellis opened her eyes. The carillon signaling Sunday services echoed across the entire east side of the harbor. She moved carefully so as not to disturb Artie and realized she actually felt clear-headed. She had expected some sort of garish nightmare, but instead she'd awakened with a greater sense of purpose. If at all possible, she was going to find the man who had made her grandmother blush, even when she didn't realize that Ellis had noticed. The letter hidden away in Gran's desk was beyond heartbreaking, there was no other word for it, but there was no point in claiming that sadness for herself just because she'd had the gall to read it. Of course, on her way home, she'd promised herself she wouldn't tell Artie, that was before she'd had some wine and fallen into a total puddle of tears while trying to parse out the tragic story. It wasn't unreasonable after that to end up blurting much more than she'd planned or at least enough so he would understand why she wanted so badly to find Gran's former lover, for that's what he'd really been. The letter had been quite clear about that, and for all the depth of her grandparents' relationship and the wonderful life they'd shared, Ellis had tried to impress upon Artie why she truly wanted Hazel to find love again.

"What're you up to so early?" Artie said.

"I'm sorry, I didn't mean to wake you."

"I heard the bells too."

"Want coffee on the deck this morning; it looks nice out there."

"I would, but I promised Chad I'd meet him for a late breakfast so he could fill me in on the music situation."

"Finally."

"And about last night, Ell, I won't discourage you, but I don't see how this can work."

"I'll muddle through, my sweet, just like always," Ellis said. "But right now, I'm up for some yogurt and watermelon and lots of coffee."

"I'll take mine to go this morning to give me strength," Artie said as he began to dress. "I've got to stop in and see Mom on the way."

"In that case, take the whole pot and I'll make another."

"Ellis."

"Arthur."

She threw on Artie's ancient tee shirt and he caught her up in a bear hug. "Are you sure you're okay?"

"Fine, really, now let me get the coffee started." She walked into the kitchen leaving him to stare at her legs and the way his shirt clung to her butt. "I know you're watching."

"I'll let you know when I get tired."

"Hurry up and get yourself in gear so I can have some peace and quiet." She dumped the exact amount of coffee into the pot and then a half-spoon more for good measure, and after she'd set the fruit and yogurt out on the deck table, she pulled his mug from the dishwasher she'd forgotten to empty out the day before.

"That's my girl," Artie said taking it out of her hand.

"Trying to make an impression on your mother?"

"I thought you liked this shirt?"

"I do; it's the pants I'm not fond of."

"Cargo pants are good for all kinds of things, especially keeping my phone and keys and stuff that you always want me to pick up for you."

"Okay, I get the message. Now, go before I rearrange your clothes."

"It's Sunday, Ell, what are you thinking?"

"You tell me," she said pinching him lovingly. She waited until he was out the door before bringing her computer out on the deck. Once she was logged in, she found the global.net email address and the contact person for the retired dancers' organization, which hopefully had not disbanded since she had no idea when the organization was founded. Suddenly, the phone rang.

"Where's the groom this morning?" asked Chad.

"On his way to you, why?"

"He's running a little late, that's all."

"Look out the store window; he's probably pulling up as we speak."

"Damn, you're good."

"I tell him that all the time…."

The phone had gone dead before she could tell him to remind Artie to get a box of thank you cards. Even Chad put in nearly a full day on Sundays during the season, and it was one of the days she preferred to shop since it was easier to find parking.

~

"Better be careful, bro, you're going to injure yourself," Artie yelled through the open truck window. Someone from Chad's staff had dropped off cartons of new books and as soon as she'd left, Artie pulled in.

"There you go again, casting aspersions on my youth and good health," Chad said while he loaded the last carton on a dolly.

Artie jumped down from the cab and said, "Don't flatter yourself—you just spend an inordinate amount of time at the Y."

"Doesn't hurt to keep fit and the ladies seem to like it," Chad said. "And don't just stand there, get the door."

"One of these days, you're going to settle down and you won't care if you get a little flabby around the middle," Artie said as he followed Chad inside.

"If that's so, why do you suck in your gut whenever Ellis walks in the room?"

"Reflex?"

"Dude, this is me you're talking to. What's in the bag?" Chad asked

"Ell's wedding gift; I had it stashed at my mom's."

"On top of everything you have to buy a separate gift."

"Protocol, and I'm not messing this up for anything."

"Does she get you one too?"

"I'm guessing, but to more serious stuff, how're you doing with the music videos?"

"You'll thank me when this is all done, believe me. But do me a favor, and at least practice dancing with Ellis just a little bit before the big day."

"Promise, now show me what you've got."

"I checked them out, read the reviews and listened to what I think is one of the smoothest sounds I've heard in a while."

"Are you bringing a dance partner with you?"

"I'm expecting to be on my own that day, why?"

"Just wondered, that's all."

"No match-making!"

"Don't know what you're talking about."

"Yeah, right," Chad said.

"So, can I give Ell the good news about the music?"

"All I have to do is break down the costs, which won't take long. I'll call you," Chad said turning back to his computer. "And, by the way, I can't wrap your wedding gift so you'll have to take it as is."

"What the hell did you buy?"

"Champagne, but I *fenagled* a yacht for your rehearsal dinner."

Artie felt his mouth drop open, "Fuck, man, this is unbelievable, how'd you manage the boat?"

"My big brother's the captain, remember the *Balboa?* She'll be in port the last two weeks in August, and he said as long as we don't wreck anything, he'd let us take it over for a night."

"I think I'm gonna kiss you."

"Don't even think about it!"

"She's not gonna believe this, and man, you just saved me a lot of hassle."

"I figured, but what can I say, I'm a sucker for a good party," Chad said. "Now go, let me finish."

Artie started to walk away and then looked back. Chad had raised his right middle finger up high while continuing to punch at the keyboard with his other hand.

~

"That errand didn't take long," Ellis said.

"Nah, just a few last-minute details, and a surprise for my girl."

"What're you talking about?"

"We've just about lined up the music."

"Just about—how is that a surprise?"

"Just one minor thing to resolve and it's all good."

"How's your mother?"

"She wasn't home."

"What *would* you do if she remarried?"

"Get drunk, and then I'd probably relax for the first time in a year," Artie said. "And speaking of drinking, Chad's giving us champagne as a wedding present."

"That's amazing, but why not surprise us?"

"Maybe just because it comes with a yacht."

"Now I know you've been smoking something."

"You haven't heard the best part," Artie said. "We're having our rehearsal dinner on said yacht with said champagne."

"Can I call him right now?"

"You can't cry like I know you're about to, but he's actually going to call here any minute because when I left him, he was just working out the cost of the band."

"I'm overwhelmed, and I had so many other things on

my mind, but this, this is unbelievably generous. Even your mother can't find fault with it."

"Ellis."

"Sorry. But take me off this giddy ledge for a minute, and tell me what you'd think of my sending an invitation to Mr. Roca."

"Let me get that phone first."

Ellis hadn't mentioned that inside her head, was the fabulous scene from Letters to Juliet only with Eduardo and Hazel as the main characters, and all made possible because of the wedding at the Colony and Hazel's very caring granddaughter. Ellis could almost see the screen credits with her name in bold letters at the end of the movie. And now, the rehearsal party on board a fabulous yacht was almost more than she could handle.

"Good news." Artie waved the phone in front of him. "He says the band you wanted has an opening, *and* are willing to pay their own way up from Boston."

"There's a *but* in there somewhere."

"We do have to put them up someplace for the night."

"Let me talk to him," Ellis said grabbing the phone. "You're my new hero!" she shouted. "And the best friend ever, and what can I say—I love you!"

Artie grabbed the phone back, "She's a little excited, right? Now all I have to do is find those guys a cheap motel near Kennebunkport to keep her this happy. Once she comes down to earth, we'll have you over for ribs so you can tell her all about Yacht *Balboa*."

"Satisfied?" Artie said hanging up.

"I know that boat."

"Yacht—it's eighty-five feet long."

"My grandfather knew the owner."

"Your grandfather knew everyone who moored in the harbor."

"Well, not everyone; I don't think he ever got to meet Jimmy Dean."

"Chad's gonna send you an attachment so you can see what she looks like."

"She is just as beautiful as she is romantic sounding, no matter how old *she* is."

"Like you are, and will be."

"Let me thank you for that," Ellis said wrapping her arms around his waist.

"Ellis."

"Arthur."

Chapter 22

The days sped by and with them, a little less hope that Marilyn would soften her stance about the ceremony's civil versus religious aspect. Then, one evening Ellis called her future mother-in-law and invited her over for an easy summer dinner and a chance to meet their wedding officiant, Judith Miller, mother of two, and die-hard mahjong player.

"Whatever made you think that would make her change her mind," Artie asked after everyone had left.

"A hunch only, but she mentioned her lack of friends when Gran had us over for lunch that day. I don't know why I happened to mention mahjong to Judith, but suddenly there was an opportunity to place your mother in a situation that might garner a new friendship and make her happy for a change."

"Well, it seems to be working, because Mom's been talking a different tune ever since."

"Gran says your mom's lonely, and I think she was right."

"Genius—it runs in the family."

"Just wait for the next big crisis; we still have to tell her about wanting to adopt."

"Please, one at a time."

"Okay, but as soon as we get back from Monhegan, I'm going to tell my folks, so be prepared."

"I've been prepared since the day I fell in love with you."

Chapter 23

After Artie left for work on Monday morning, Ellis called her father just to make sure she wasn't needed and had been given his blessing to stay home and complete her own project, which he thought was wedding related. He asked after Fred Treadwell, and that triggered Ellis's memory of her last conversation with Millie and the unexpected comments: "You and your grandad were like two peas in a dory, but that doesn't mean Hazel couldn't use some love in her life again." Ellis blushed all over again just thinking of Millie's follow up. "I know it's not easy picturing a grandparent between the sheets," she'd said while Ellis stared open-mouthed at the dated expression and its implications. But at least, Millie had agreed to becoming Ellis's spy and co-conspirator. And now, as she unrolled the large parchment, Ellis thought of Jeanie who had managed to form a crush on Peter Hamilton. His portfolio had been so spectacular, that she'd made him swear he would take her wedding pictures one day, and then Ellis saw a spark fly between them. It was actually perfect; this could make Chad jealous for sure, especially since Peter had agreed to come up and take the photographs during their rehearsal party. Ellis had to admit, once those awful chemo sessions were over and his color restored along with his natural weight, he was rather a hunk.

Ellis dug into the blanket chest where she kept the folder with all the found family names, and her fingers brushed against one of the sample wedding favors that the company in Rockland had sent. In the end, she and Artie had decided on tiny wooden boxes to be hand painted with her favorite lighthouse image as well as their names and the date of the wedding in script along the bottom. It had been one of the last snags in their decision-making, and an irritant only, but it felt good to have it out of the way. She looked at the clock; there was plenty of time for her project, so she brought everything to the outdoor table and began the process of sorting and adding what she'd gathered during the last visit to her grandmother's:

David H. son of W. Scott, married Olive B.
David, son of Andrew, married Sarah T.
Andrew, son of John, married Nancy D (cousin?)
John, son of Timothy, married Abigail W.
Timothy, son of John, married to Sarah J.
John, son of Samuel, married to Ruth B.
Samuel, son of John, married to Hannah F.

It was one of the most difficult tasks she'd ever undertaken, and just as before, she found herself mired in the confusion of tracking backward and the repetitiveness of all their names; nothing about this project was going to be straightforward. It certainly wasn't any easier on the Ellis side of the chart either, except she'd made the fun connection between them and President John Adams. *Six degrees of separation,* she thought except it was more like twenty-six in this case. The Beane side was all tangled up too, and it seemed the only way to untangle most of the men who shared the name Timothy, just like the Ellis family, was to start with the ones named Charles and then those named James. There was no easy way to handle any of this branch either, and the simplest format was to find out when the various men died and where possible, the full names of their spouses. So far, she'd had one lucky break when she uncovered photos of headstones in Middlesex County, Massachusetts, and even in one case, Suffolk County, England, but that was a female ancestor whom she couldn't attach to anyone other than a brother.

But now Ellis had the Bible in her possession—no more sneaky visits to Ocean Point—and all that was left was to keep it safe until she could make an appointment with a conservator of rare books in Portland that she'd found through a restorer of fine prints. She hated keeping secrets from her grandmother and had nearly told her about wanting to name a boy child Oliver, but that would have opened up all those other parental doors. She and Artie were the right age, with the right incomes and family supportiveness, at least on Ellis's side, so they both felt it wasn't prudent to wait much longer to begin the process. It might take years before they found a newborn, because this was the one thing about which they'd been of like minds. Maybe for a second or third child, they'd seek older, but she wanted to experience the whole messy lot of infancy, everything other women complained about while later saying they wouldn't have missed one moment of it. And without telling anyone, she'd written to her brother about the boys she would be grateful to raise, boys like him and her dad and her new husband. Boys who would go on to be good husbands and sons themselves and hopefully never have to set foot on any foreign soil in the throes of war ever again.

Jake had been away so long that Ellis had nearly forgotten the things they'd done together. He'd taught her to swim in Damariscotta Lake because that gave him a reason to see the cheerleader whose parents had a summer cabin there. He'd given Ellis her driving lessons when their father had scared her witless with all the dos and don'ts of driving. And Jake had escorted her to her first prom when she didn't have a date. And now, all she wanted to do was give him hope, and the will to keep going so he might one day see a little niece or nephew. He was on his second tour and had missed so much already that she wasn't sure how he'd adjust when he finally made it back home. She could no longer watch the tributes to fallen soldiers.

The day slipped by and Ellis plodded through until she realized the sun had started its decline. Twilight was the magic hour and the ribbons of colors could be seen in the distance as they bounced off the water and onto the wall of stones at the base of their lawn. The papers in front of her had disappeared among the violet shadows.

Packing everything up, she went into the kitchen and poured herself a glass of wine; that new buttery Chardonnay was perfection and definitely going to stay on the shelves at Berman's Provisions. In preparation for the wedding, she had done all the buying for the month of August—one more thing crossed off her list—and tomorrow morning, Millie was scheduled to meet with Hazel. And as Millie had said, "to test the waters", whatever that meant, but Ellis was already biting her fingernails.

"Stop," Artie yelled as he walked through the door.

Ellis pulled her index finger out of her mouth and said, "I'm just anxious." She wasn't certain Millie would be able to finesse the conversation though she had insisted she was far better equipped to converse about the elderly in waiting—for anything—because not only were they the best of friends, but the exact same age and apparently, Millie, had also had a brush with temptation once upon a time.

Chapter 24

Hazel spotted Millie's dusty black Jeep as soon as she pulled into Mama D's nearly empty parking lot. They'd timed their meet for what they liked to call the magic hour. It was after the happy-to-be-on-vacationers left to board the whale-watching boats or the schooner *Eastwind*, and before the ever-familiar locals were due to arrive for lunch. It was the best time of day for Millie in particular, whose voice could, if given the opportunity, bounce off the kitschy memorabilia all the while her hands fluttered with her own answers.

Hazel was already second-guessing her own mood: the wedding date was fast approaching; the days of summer rapidly disappearing, and everyone was trying to cram everything in because as she always swore, Maine had the shortest summers known to man. But of course, she would be wrong. No one could quantify anything anymore thanks to climate change. *And there you go again.* She adjusted her posture, not wanting to hang onto the rhetoric she'd just heard on the car radio because this was not the spot even though Millie was a self-declared political junky. There were other things to address on this fine summer morning, she thought as she spotted her friend looking leggy as ever in tapered pants. She was standing by the front window, cup in hand and looking out at the inner harbor. Unlike their ordinary jabber on all harbor topics, Hazel had been having a tough time justifying what was really on her mind these days: fall, and in particular, the fall of '63. "This was a nice idea," Hazel said as she approached the coffee urns.

"I thought so too." Mille said. "Good thing we both love breakfast for lunch, because I took the liberty of ordering for you."

Hazel never complained—she loved the gluten free egg sandwiches—but as soon as they settled at a table, she asked, "How's Fred doing?"

"He's such a baby," Millie replied. "It's only a case of overdoing it in the yard since he never listens, but if you don't mind my saying, you're not looking so good either."

"I've just had a lot on my mind and haven't had a good night's sleep in days. Seems like I'm up at somewhere around two every morning, and then I have to read myself back to sleep."

"At least you can turn the light on whenever you like. Fred just grumbles and flounces and turns his back on me, noisily."

"Married life, right?"

"Ever think about getting married again, or have I

already asked you?"

"About a hundred times, Millie, but that's okay." Maybe this was the right time to say what had truly been bothering her, Hazel thought. They'd become the best of friends and she was probably the only one who might get the way Hazel's mind worked. "Did you ever feel like you were disappearing, you know, getting so old, no one notices you anymore?"

"Isn't that just loneliness talking?"

"Probably, but being at the Colony made me remember the young woman I'd been and the dreams I had, and now, I'm just empty."

"Maybe you should get a dog."

"Oh, sweet Millie, you really are the perfect friend."

"Or a vibrator, if it's that type of loneliness."

"Millie Treadwell! What book have you been reading?"

"It wasn't salacious or anything; just an autobiography by a movie star older than us even, who candidly stated that using one was why she looked so youthful. Of course, I'd die if I had one and Fred happened to find it."

"And…"

"And, sex is supposed to keep us healthy; you of all people should know that. You're always following the latest health trends and you're the only one of our friends who still routinely does her exercises."

"This is not how I thought this conversation would go,

but if you must know, I have been yearning a little lately, if that's the right word."

"You're not in the grave yet; let's find you a man," Millie said.

"The whole idea of doing that makes me cringe, and why do you look like you swallowed a canary?" Hazel could not imagine a man in this town who could make her feel even half as good as the mere thought of Eduardo had already done. "Besides, I wouldn't know where to begin."

"What about Harry Ryan? I see how he hangs around after book club on the off chance you'll talk with him."

"I talk to him all the time, but he's not my type."

"Which is?"

"Someone who likes to dance perhaps?"

"Since when do you dance, or for that matter, when do any of us?" Millie squirmed and sipped her coffee.

"But maybe we could if we had a good reason."

"Not my Fred, no way, no how. Have you ever looked at those two left feet, a size fourteen at least?"

"Millie, you'd be lost without him and you know it."

"I know, I shouldn't complain, he's a good husband."

"Can you keep a secret?"

"Did I ever tell anyone when you bought that condominium before you'd even mentioned it to your family?"

"And I really appreciated that."

"So, what's the big secret this time?"

"You're going to think I've gone over the edge, but I promise I haven't. There was a man once, a *really* long time ago, before I'd married John, and I haven't thought about him in over fifty years, and suddenly I can't stop thinking about him. He once made me feel like anything was possible."

"Where is he?"

"Dead for all I know."

"Then why torture yourself; isn't there any way you can find out?"

"I haven't a clue and it seems so out of my comfort zone to try."

"If you ask me, you'll just have to expand your zone."

"Are you sure you're all right; you seem awfully antsy this morning," Hazel said just as the waitress placed their orders on the table. "If nothing else, here's to expanding my waistline."

"Hah, not you, but at least this whatever it is, hasn't ruined your appetite. Then I'd have to rethink our friendship."

They sat there talking as always, way beyond the time when the lunch crowd came and went and were still talking as the tables were cleared and the floor about to be swept. "How do we do this?" Hazel said. "It never fails to amaze me that we can talk half the day away without a nod or wink to whatever else has to be done."

"All the while we've been gabbing, I've been running through my feeble brain for available men and have drawn a complete blank."

"Please don't ask me to check out one of those awful dating sites, even if there is one for people our age."

"You could ask Ellis to help."

"Not on your life!"

"How are their wedding plans coming along?"

"Good, the last time I checked. Her dress is breathtaking, and Artie walks around looking like he can hardly wait for it all to be over. How well do you know his mother?"

"Marilyn? By reputation only, but Fred knew Arthur from Rotary."

"Poor Janet, she's found her nemesis. Marilyn is giving her a run for her money and our Ellis is caught in the middle."

"Rumor has it that Marilyn pushed her own daughter into marriage with some financial guru from Portland, some heir to one of the scions of a hotel franchise."

"She did mention that she never sees her daughter anymore, maybe that's the reason," Hazel said. "Not that I'm into rumors.

"Fred told me once that Marilyn was a little tyrant, and I told him he didn't know what a real tyrant was, and you should've seen the look he gave me."

"You're too funny."

"I know, he says that too. But listen, let's go shopping before you get caught up in more wedding stuff. I need to pick out something to wear on our cruise."

"I nearly forgot—the *Viking*?"

"Yep, and I can't wait, and fall is the perfect time so I won't have to miss out on a thing here in the harbor," Millie said. "Of course, when we get back, I'll have to buy more new clothes because they serve all those fattening wieners and beer."

"Maybe I should find a singles cruise." Hazel picked up the tab for them both and steered Millie out the door before they started on another topic.

"By the way, I sent in my RSVP, but I'm not sure if Fred will go; you know how he is about sitting with a bunch of women."

"I'm very fond of Fred, but the decision's up to both of you."

"I was just thinking that maybe without a distraction and my keen eye, I can find you someone to sweep you onto the dancefloor."

"You're both on the guest list so it's your choice."

"Trust me, he'd enjoy a Saturday without me trying to figure out what needs doing around the house," Millie said as they walked to their cars. "Pick a date for our little shopping excursion and call me later. And, by the way, I still haven't seen the sapphire blue dress I've heard so much about."

"You can see it when you pick me up; it's your turn to drive."

Chapter 25

Out on the deck of the Blue Moon Café, Ellis tried to compartmentalize the earful she'd gotten from dear Millie, though neither of them had come up with a solid idea for handling Hazel's dilemma...yet. But as she sat contemplating, Ellis had the strangest sense that the fog was swaying—flirtatiously—lifting one corner and then another across the expanse of the harbor, like a dancer's skirt shooing away the bothersome gray that had all but buried the moored boats. And that reminded her that she and Millie had flirted with the idea of calling Eduardo directly, which they then considered could shock someone of his age into an unforeseen condition. Ellis scrunched down into her fleece jacket and put her face up to the damp and tasted the dew on her tongue and wondered what she'd say to Jeanie whose keys she could hear jangling as she walked up the ramp.

"Can't see a thing out there."

"You're not supposed to, and I love it," Ellis said.

"And you asked me here why?" Jeanie said.

"To bring you up to date on everything before you go to work."

"I have a phone."

"Very funny; I just wanted some company, that's all."

"Do you want another coffee?"

"You go ahead, I'm good with this," Ellis said tapping her cup. More coffee wouldn't help. She kept thinking about what Millie had said about yearnings, but it wasn't a word Ellis normally associated with her grandmother, or maybe it was more about what would that look like at this stage having to do with Eduardo. After all, he too had to be around the same age, and if Ellis compared him to someone like Fred, this Eduardo might not be quite the knight in shining armor she'd hoped for. Then again, maybe it wasn't about looks at all. Ellis laughed; Jeanie would so love this topic, if only she could share it. But in truth, that might not happen until the time when they would both be at Mama D's sharing a table and talking about aging the way her grandmother and Millie apparently did.

"Okay, what's the latest?"

Ellis squinted into the gray and looked back at Jeanie's quizzical expression, and her best intentions tanked. "I'm trying to find my Gran's old lover!"

"What the hell?"

"I just can't wait until we're as old as Gran and Millie."

"For what?"

"To remember what it's like to want someone so badly

after their gone!"

"Are you baiting me on purpose; get to the point!"

"My grandmother needs to find the man she met at the Colony in 1963, and I intend to make that happen, with Millie's help of course. But I was about to burst if I didn't share this with you. I thought about it all the way here, drove through town romanticizing the fog the way I do, and then remembered that question about what happens when a tree falls in the forest with no one to witness it, and I knew I couldn't hold this in any longer."

"How do you come up with all this nonsense for something as ubiquitous as stupid fog, and more importantly, why have you waited all this time to tell me?"

"You get depressed in the fog."

"Not that, the other stuff, about Hazel and Millie, but don't' just keep me hanging here waiting for this wetness to ruin my hair, which I'll have you know looked pretty great when I left the house."

Ellis leaned closer and began at the beginning or at least the parts involving Eduardo that she'd gleaned from her grandmother's letter to Sloane.

~

"I'm dumbstruck."

"Join the party."

"What's next, then."

"I'm sending him an invitation; it seems the only logical thing to do, but I'm on shaky ground here."

"More like volcanic, Ellis—erupting any minute volcanic."

"Now you see why I wanted a little handholding this morning."

"Look, I can't stay much longer, but we're not finished here," Jeanie said. "And by the way, I've been fielding calls from some of the older folks who don't really like using a gift registry and I've directed those people to your Grandmother. Anything else gets run by your mom."

"Millie said she's got a teeth-cleaning scheduled; please don't let on that you know."

"We'll talk about my mother instead; she loves that Millie's going to be at the reception. Did I ever tell you that Mom makes manicotti for her and Fred on request?"

"She's good for Gran."

"And I'm good for you, and don't you forget it," Jeanie said. "And before I forget, is there anything new with your future mother-in-law, or should I say, anything printable?"

"Bonded we're not, but Artie says she's beginning to refer to us as *her kids*, which is a start, right?"

"Speaking of kids, have you told your families about wanting to adopt?"

"Not yet. We've decided to wait until after the

wedding dust settles. There's a lot to consider—the least of which is how and where. It's all the other nonsense that bogs me down if I think too hard. Marilyn, for instance, will find a way to demean the idea because it won't be *her* flesh and blood. My folks will care more about the things that can go wrong in private adoptions, and Gran will want to pay for whichever we decide. She's done too much already."

"At least you don't have to decide right away; your calendar being a little full right now. And, speaking of, my mom wants to know if you and Artie would like a pan of lasagna; she made extra."

"That's really nice of her; just please don't tell her I'm still off carbs."

"Italians are never off carbs; are you crazy?"

"You've gotta go or you really will be late."

"Can't help myself; there's just too much for me to digest."

"My mother gets apoplectic each time she realizes that Marilyn won't go away like a bad house guest. She's stuck with that woman for as long as they both shall live, and she doesn't know how to embrace it."

"My cousin Nino had the same issue with his mother-in-law, couldn't stand the intrusion into their lives, so he refused to be anywhere she was expected to be. His wife finally got tired of attending functions alone, so she finally told her mother to butt out. Now the mother-in-law won't have anything to do with the family unless it's a really big function where she and Nino can avoid each other."

"Jeanie, this is Boothbay Harbor; we can't spit without hitting someone we know; how is my mother going to avoid Marilyn, or vice versa?"

"Just a thought."

"Me thinks we'd better come up with something more appropriate, but in the meantime, what are you wearing for the rehearsal dinner?"

"My little black dress and my slinky sandals and my best smile."

"You found out his date canceled, didn't you?"

"Artie did happen to let that slip when I ran into him at Hannaford's, and now that I know Peter's coming, well…"

"Give it your best shot, that's all I can say." Ellis picked up both their cups and brought them to the plastic bin on the deck.

"It's about the only shot I have left and I'm going for it!" Jeanie said following her out to the street." Besides, out on a yacht, under the stars, how could it get any better than that."

"We'll be forever grateful to Chad for this one."

"I'd be forever grateful if he gives me what I long for."

"Now I know it's time to leave, and besides I've gotta check in at Aura's to see about their shipment of nail colors."

"Call you later."

Ellis had parked up the hill not far from the hair salon, and Jeanie had managed to find a spot in front of the bookstore. *Subtle she is not,* Ellis thought.

Chapter 26

Hazel thought about all the times throughout the years that she'd bitched about the fog. Today, it was truly apropos of her mood and she didn't know what to do with herself. She couldn't go walking, she didn't feel like cooking, which she often did on the weekends so she wouldn't have to figure out what to eat every day. And, she didn't particularly feel like talking to anyone. *Melancholia,* she thought. *Deep sadness or gloom.* Well, she and old Webster were on the same page there. How had she gotten so mired in all this nonsensical thinking about Eduardo and where would she be able to deposit this form of unhappiness. *You can't really lose what you never actually had,* she mused as she sipped at her third cup of coffee. Even Millie was acting strangely. Hazel had helped her find something in the wedding registry that Ellis would like and Millie had adored the new blue dress, and they'd gone shopping for her travel outfit all the while Millie had kept looking at Hazel as if she had something on her face that needed washing off. Maybe one of the planets was in retrograde or something. *What about your happy place,* she thought? It was the perfect weather to wander the stacks at the Boothbay Harbor Memorial Library. Certainly, they would have a few how-to books on aging gracefully. "Hah!" Her voice bounced off the walls. Before she'd lost her spunk, she thought that kind of grace applied to eating well and exercising and keeping all her teeth in her mouth. Now, she wasn't so sure.

Hazel opened the door and stuck her hand out. A pair of jeans, which according to Millie, Hazel still looked good in, would be perfect for a day like this. She added the new cotton pullover that Millie had talked her into buying to make herself feel better about spending so much money on travel clothes. After checking herself in the mirror, Hazel threw on her bright green rain jacket and headed for her car.

Once in town, it appeared the weather hadn't spoiled anyone else's day, which was emphasized by bright ponchos and raingear bobbing in and out of the mist. The metered parking lots were full and all the spaces in front of the library were taken. Hazel drove around a few times and finally ended up near the Tugboat Inn just as someone in a big sedan was maneuvering his way out. The mist started to feel more like rain so she pulled a floppy hat out of the glove box and plopped it on her head. Fashionable she was not, but since it was Saturday, it didn't matter because she'd be getting her hair done this afternoon before going home.

"Look at all of you in your bright colors," Hazel exclaimed as she passed the counter. The library volunteers had obviously dressed to combat the gloom too, but they hardly looked up from their sorting and cataloging, and Hazel noted that the librarian's door was closed. So, it was down to business, she thought as she headed upstairs to the reference material. She started to walk between those stacks when it hit her that what she really wanted for a day like this, was a mystery novel, and they were on the first floor. She had absolutely devoured the Donna Leon books set in Venice and had already gone through all of her favorite Maine mystery writers (catalogued B thru F in the large main floor room) and had only just begun reading a new author's work. Walking along the aisle marked M-P, she ran her finger across the tabs until she found what she wanted and then brought the book into the small side room with its comfortable chairs, thinking she could easily kill enough time until her hair appointment. Then, she intended to take herself out for a late lunch within walking distance from the salon. Besides the fact that she'd just seen Millie, this was not a Southport kind of day. *Well, that's it,* she thought, the day is planned. She'd even grab a couple of DVDs while she was here, and then the entire night was planned too.

~

An hour and a half later, Hazel left the beauty shop feeling rather perky until she stepped in a puddle and splashed dirty water all over her tennis shoes and cold water fell from the rain gutter above and slipped down the back of her neck and wet down her newly styled do. *So much for looking good again.* Hazel rushed to her car; all thought of a lunch out somewhere gone. Instead, she'd head home to fix something from whatever was left in the freezer. *Pea soup—Eduardo.* Would she ever stop remembering, and did she really want to? Once she was behind the wheel, she looked at herself in the rearview mirror and wondered what others saw even as she chastised herself for such vanity. Without the sun, or the fuss she had gone to at the Colony, her skin looked absolutely blah. Her eyes were red-rimmed from so many new restless nights, and the parentheses around her mouth seemed to have deepened overnight. The Mowry money she'd come into would have allowed for a big makeover, but she always remembered those stories in the movie magazines available at the beauty shop, and the stitching and stapling required and the healing time, and her stomach would turn over if she even considered choosing the knife over some very expensive skin products. And, who was looking at her anyway? Millie's notion of Hazel's getting out there and dating again, seemed preposterous. How do you date in your seventies anyway: make polite conversation over dinner; walk arm-and-arm to the movies and share a large tub of popcorn and pray that none of the kernels get stuck in that tooth you had repaired last month. Or maybe, sit on hard boulders out at Ocean Point until your ass is frozen and numbed even in the summer because your sit bones no longer had proper cushioning, and your date, whoever that might be, would more than likely be suffering in a similar way. Was that really what she hoped to do for the rest of her days? And, what was so wrong with widowhood anyhow. She had her schedules the way she liked; she could choose not to get dressed for an entire day if she didn't feel like it; she could read all night long in the middle of the bed if that made her happy, and talk to herself as loudly as she pleased. But she'd no sooner relinquished all those thoughts into the air when she remembered the Colony Hotel ballroom and the way her body had responded to some subliminal force of nature, a primal sensation that most likely made the world turn for anyone who'd experienced a similar call at least once in their lives. She began to cry, even before she'd started the car, tears were wetting her cheeks and making thin rivulets through the film of moisturizer she always wore. *This was not the way this day was supposed to go.* She pulled a tissue from her purse and put the car in gear.

By the time she got home, Hazel knew exactly what she needed: *Solo por hoy — Only for Today.* She'd found it on

Amazon along with a recording of *Tango Argentino*. They were the only CDs in her small collection of tapes. With this music, Eduardo could again become the personification of all that he loved, and what in a short period of time, he had tried to teach her—the ways of the dance—a pulling in and retreating from, movements indicating a history between lovers when in fact it was often performed by strangers on a stage or even in the small clubs of Europe. Relationships were not a prerequisite to a great tango; learning to feel the music with your entire being, was. Thoughts of Eduardo had all but consumed her days and nights since she'd returned from the Colony; now it was essential that she step into the dream she had artfully orchestrated to match the bigger-than-life sound filling up her home. The music would soon caress her skin, and if she was very lucky, it would smooth away the worry that had taken hold—the fear of dying without knowing what might have happened if he hadn't stopped the music.

She thought of Sloane and her ability to open her heart to love no matter what. Hazel listened for the clues as the music throbbed, hoping to find her inner *tanguera* once more. How exquisite it would be to awaken all those feelings she'd kept hidden, even from herself.

She went to the phone and called Millie.

Chapter 27

"Are you free tonight?"

"What's wrong, Millie?" Ellis said.

"Hazel needs an intervention; we have to tell her what we're up to."

"Why, what happened?"

"Whatever it is, she needs a friend, and in this case, I think she needs to know what you and I have been planning," Millie said. "She was uncharacteristically babbling about this music she wanted me to hear and then she turned up the volume and held the phone out for me to listen...and I recognized it!"

"What was it?"

"Tango."

"Uh oh."

"Ever since she told me about what happened at that hotel, I've been trying my best to figure out the dance steps using a U-Tube clip, but trust me, it's really intimate...if it's done right.

"Cheek to cheek, thigh over and leg under and hardly a space between them; that's just the woman's part. The man holds her with fierce intensity, and seems to direct her moves with a twist of a wrist and his eyes say words no one hears, and right now I think I'm getting very warm. I used to watch every time Max danced with that ice skater on *Dancing with the Stars;* talk about steamy! I thought I'd have died and gone to heaven if Fred ever danced with me that way. Naturally, I just drank my wine and watched as he complained that men never danced *or* dressed like that, but he never took his eyes away from the screen."

"Now I really am dumbfounded, but I can change my plans; Jeanie will understand." *Especially since she now knows,* Ellis thought. "I hope this doesn't blow up in my face, but I sent an email to that address you gave me, and attached a scanned copy of the wedding invitation since Gran's name is also there, so whatever she's going through tonight will be worse if he doesn't respond. Oops, Artie just walked in the door; I'll meet you there in an hour."

"What's up?"

"Just Millie catching me up."

"Hope your plans for tonight haven't changed; Chad and I are meeting some of the guys for drinks."

"I was just about to call Jeanie to tell her I'm going over to Gran's for a little while."

"Everything okay over there?"

"I'm really not sure, but Millie wants me to meet her there."

"Sounds ominous."

"When all this is over, do you think we could learn to tango?"

"Not that again."

"I can't help it; Millie, of all people, was just describing what it's like and it sounds pretty amazing…just sayin'."

"Chad says I need to learn some basic steps for the reception, which I do believe will take me the entire time we have left from now until."

"Baby steps, then. I'm a patient person."

"So, you say, and speaking of babies, are we still on the same page about when to break the news?"

"Absolutely. And are you sure Chad's flying solo for the rehearsal party?"

"So far."

"Then let me fix a quick salad so we can both do what needs doing tonight," Ellis said. "Oh, I forgot to mention that I sent an email to Mr. Roca. I gave him Gran's married name so at least he'd be able to Google it, which would probably pull up the newspaper article and photo that ran after Gramps died…the one that showed Gran cutting the ribbon for the new rec center."

"Forgot to mention?" Artie said. "I guess it's official, then, we've crossed the line from meddling to interfering."

"I don't think of it that way at all."

~

Without clearing away the dishes, she kissed Artie and shooed him out the door. Then she double-checked her emails and slipped on a sweater and locked up. If nothing else, Gran would allow her to vent all she wanted about Marilyn and her latest edict that the two mothers shouldn't wear corsages. She'd said it was about her allergies (again) but Ellis was beginning to believe it was that old control issue rearing its ugly head. But at least everything else had fallen into place. No wedding showers, no bachelor parties, just the amazing yacht extravaganza to herald in their wedding. Less cost for everyone and that was a Maine thing too, Ellis thought just as she pulled into the Ocean Point parking space.

"What are you doing here?" Hazel asked.

"Millie said to meet her."

"What are you two up to?"

"Let's wait for her okay, and besides I wanted to bring you up to speed on something else, in person."

"Your mother has already regaled me with all things wrong with Marilyn, and it's not nearly as bad as you thought, but this is not the right time for me to rehash it."

"Are you ill?"

"No, Ellis, just...oh, what can I say, feeling foolish," Hazel said. "There's Millie now."

Ellis watched as her grandmother went to the door and then she heard Millie mumble something before they both walked into the living room. "What have you two done?" Hazel asked.

"Don't get your dander up, Hazel, and just listen, please."

"Gran, it's all my fault, but I talked Millie into helping me find Eduardo."

"You did what?"

"Hazel, I'm the one who convinced her we had to do something; you're too young and vibrant to be fading on the vine, and besides, just think of that wonderful music and how much it meant to you," Millie said arcing her hand back toward the CD player.

"This is ludicrous. How could you possibly find him, and what if he doesn't want to be found...by me!"

"We're kinda leaving that up to the gods right now, Gran, but I did find a retired dancer's organization online, and Millie got his email address from one of the surviving members, and then I invited him to come to my wedding."

"Just like that; he's supposed to go to a perfect stranger's wedding; what were you thinking?"

"I know you're really pissed, Hazel, but she did the only thing we could do."

"And, I managed to find a photo from the newspaper so he could see how beautiful you still are."

"And if he turns up and he's ugly as sin and thinks he's going to move in with a wealthy old widow, what then?"

"You're not that old, and I don't think you'd have been craving his attention all these weeks, if you thought that for a moment, Hazel."

Suddenly, they were all hugging and crying as only women who read too many books and watched too many love stories could do. "All right, girls," Hazel said. "Let's see where this takes us. Ellis, get out the wine please, I think we have a lot to talk about, and you, Millie, need a lesson in tango music and I have the perfect song right over here.

Ellis left them in the living room and as she got out the glasses, she also pulled her phone out of her pocket and snapped a picture of them from a distance, laughing through their tears like a couple of schoolgirls, and Ellis knew no matter what the future brought, this was the way she wanted her friendship with Jeanie to unfold. "Here we are," Ellis said as she set the wine down in front of them.

"I understand that this big yacht is going to solve all of Artie's issues about the rehearsal dinner," Hazel said.

"It's so perfect, and it keeps Marilyn off our backs about expenses."

"I can't remember what Fred's parents shelled out for ours, but it was awful."

"Rubber chicken?" Hazel asked.

"Exactly."

"Well, we're having a smattering of fancy hors

d'oeuvres and mini-sliders and ribs to soak up the champagne that Chad gifted us, which embarrassed Marilyn so much, she shelled out a check for the honeymoon."

"Don't worry, she can afford it. Fred said Arthur had a huge retirement package and also a hefty insurance policy."

"You're as bad as Janet."

"Well, it's the truth, and Ellis has a right to know what makes that woman tick."

"And she also has to learn her way around the prickly issue of making sure they're on the same page when it comes to her son; that's all she really cares about," Hazel said.

"How can you be so sure, Gran?"

"Just so happens, your mother and Marilyn and I had our own little pre-wedding celebration on Janet's porch, which was always my favorite spot in the old house. It's amazing what a little tequila does to loosen a person's lips."

"Since when does my mother drink tequila?"

"Not her, Marilyn; turns out it's her one guilty pleasure, at least that's what she confessed to, and what I haven't yet said, is that she thinks your gown is stunning."

"You're kidding!"

"God's truth, and with her lips loosened, she said she'd

inquired about Chad's brother and it turns out he's divorced, and you should have seen how she cozied up to your mother."

"I don't believe it after that business about the corsages; you're just saying this to make me feel better."

"Not at all; they're riding together in the limo too."

"Remind me to stock up on tequila for Fred's sake of course, and speaking of pleasure, you said you wanted us to hear a new piece of music?"

"Something we need to know, Millie?"

"As a matter of fact, I've been watching U-Tube and I like what I saw."

"If Eduardo has the ability and the nerve to actually show up, maybe we'll show you how it's done."

"So, you did learn more than you let on," Ellis said.

"A little."

"Now you're talking," Millie said. "But let's not get our hopes up too high; he's still in his seventies."

"So, I gather," Hazel said. "And yet, neither of you think I'm too old to be feeling like this."

"Oops."

"Oops, is right," Hazel said changing discs. "Pour me another glass please, Ellis."

"That's from *Mr. & Mrs. Smith*," Ellis yelled. "I loved that movie!"

"Well this was a little bonus for ordering a few other

items; maybe there is something to this online shopping after all," Hazel said. "And this is more the pace that I recall from 1963, but who knows, maybe it was all in my imagination and I've let it blow all out of proportion."

"That's just cold feet talking, my friend."

"I can't take anymore," Ellis said. "I'm going home and put on some music and hope that Artie comes home sober enough to dance."

"From what I'm told, maybe the liquor would do him some good in that department," Hazel said.

"Marilyn must have blabbed, but I'm leaving before I need to call a cab," Ellis said. "I'll call you both tomorrow!"

Hazel walked her to the door, and said, "You did a foolish thing, but whatever happens, I'll always be grateful you loved me this much."

"To the moon and back," Ellis said hugging her goodbye.

Hazel walked back in and said, "Turned out to be quite a night after all."

"My turn to hug it out and leave you to your dreams; Fred's waiting." Millie said walking Hazel back toward the door. "This has been good for Ellis too; maybe it'll ease her way through the quagmire we call marriage."

"Do you think he'll come?"

"It's my greatest hope, but even if he doesn't, you have

blossomed before my eyes, the Hazel I've always known, and I'm proud of you."

"Oh, Millie, you are the most loyal friend in the world."

"Let me get out of here before we dissolve into one of our infamous crying jags."

Hazel closed the door and slipped off her shoes; the rooms were cool and she was now wide awake. Putting the new CD on loud enough to hear through the screen door, she went outside and back to the freedom of her thoughts: concertina and bandoneon, and the way Eduardo had demonstrated with his body what happens when those instruments are joined by the violins. She looked into the dark and tried to picture him, her body trying to wake up to the tempo she once cherished—one quick beat, two slow beats—the steps she hadn't been able to recover at the Colony without the actual accompaniment. Without his presence, she was forced to imagine the silent conversations and the burning heat the dance only insinuated on a stage. She could never forget the temperature their bodies had achieved and where the end of the dance had taken them. *It may never happen again,* she thought, but nothing could stop her from the pleasure this music would continue to give her. She walked closer to the water and was suddenly reminded of John and their usual after-event conversations, which was yet another part of learning to be alone. Right about now, he would have poured them a dram of brandy while they rehashed the pleasures or dullness at the end of whatever had spurred them to such conversations. *A night very much like this.* And if it was a really warm night, they would sit on the veranda overlooking the harbor lights until their glasses were empty and their voices dropped off.

Hazel shook her head, and took another sip of her wine, and before going inside, stopped to take a good, long look at the stars. *Where's everyone tonight.* The sky winked and the planets stared with bright abandon as if to let her know that she'd be okay on her own if that's what was meant to be. And remind her that she too would eventually become part of the night sky, or so she hoped, just as she hoped that time was a long way away. Nearby, the water rose and fell and brushed the rocks, teasing the night along with its own musical rendition of love. And for the first time in a long time, she was remembering the most precious of things without a heavy heart—the friends, relatives and a husband who'd brought her this far. Suddenly, the musical tease ended in a crashing cymbal of water against the shore, and she realized how heavy-minded she'd gotten in the short time she'd been outside. Peering up one last time, she said, "Good night John, good night Sloane, good night moon." Hazel then poured the last of the wine on the ground and went back inside, her bare feet taking an extra beat on the wooden floor, keeping time with the new CD. Life was good.

Chapter 28

On the following Saturday, decorations of all sorts were fighting for space on Jeanie's small table.

"Will these lights do?" Jeanie asked.

"They'll look like twinkling stars," Ellis said. "And the clamshell dishes I brought over are perfect for holding nuts and those little goldfish crackers Chad likes so much. And, you know we have to keep him happy after all of this."

"I know how to make him happy, but he just won't let me."

"Have you taken a head count for the party?"

"Are you changing the subject?" Jeanie asked. "Is Chad's brother single?"

"Jeanie, one at a time please."

"Just asking, and the head count so far is twenty-three."

"He's not great husband material; he's always moving from port to port.

"And a girl in every one?"

"Maybe."

"I heard Artie's sister's here."

"She and money-pockets are getting a divorce, so we won't have to put up with his bullshit," Ellis said. "And now I'm not the only one who'll be in their family with that dirty word on her résumé."

"I guess that's something, then," Jeanie said. "The guys are over at Brown's keeping a stiff upper lip at the thought of losing their leader; after that, they may fall like dominos."

"You wish."

"I do wish, because I'm ready to get married. And I want what you have with Artie."

"I need to do better with his mother."

"Maybe she'll find another husband; she's still young."

"I think she might be the one with her sights set on the captain."

"And another one bites the dust."

"I have an idea, why don't you show me your new shoes while we wait for the girls."

"They'd better hurry with that pizza, I'm starving," Jeanie said. "Maybe Artie's brother is the right age for Marilyn."

"Pretty soon, we're going to need a score card to keep up with you."

"Nah, I've about given up."

"Did I tell you Gran's hired half the fleet of limousines to ferry us all to Kennebunkport."

"I wish she was my grandmother."

"I have to admit she is pretty cool. But I'm sort of caught between a rock and a hard place with missing Gramps and hoping the dancer shows up on the twenty-eighth."

"Did you get into trouble about that?"

"Almost, but there was this glimmer of excitement afterward; she almost looked like the girl in her photograph, but you have to promise me you won't tell anyone else about this."

"I swear, but I did tell my mom about the whole girls in blue thing.

"It was such a subconscious choice; we've always loved blue, but I never thought how much it would mean to her," Ellis said. "I was also told I'm becoming like my great-grandmother, Midge."

"Loud?"

"No, more like having the language of a seafaring sailor."

"Ha, I never noticed."

"That's because we're a lot alike," Ellis said. "And there's our pizza delivery."

"Let me get some paper plates and a soft drink for our little mother."

"It'll be fine, Jeanie, she's just hormonal."

"Then I'm never having kids."

"Jeanie, you're Italian."

Chapter 29

Normally, throughout the summer months yachts of all types and sizes, having cruised the Med or the Caribbean, would find their way to the shores of Maine. Many ending up in Boothbay Harbor, either moored out or tied up dockside at Brown's Wharf, depending on their size and the number of adult toys they carried. And now, four days before the wedding, the Yacht *Balboa* was cozied up to the wharf, its tiny lights blazing as if it were about to enter the lighted boat parade instead of it being the setting for a wedding rehearsal. And like the arriving guests, the gleaming white, eighty-five-footer sparkled with anticipation. Ellis had taken an earlier tour, surprised by the layout and finding that because of its age and style, it had a homier feel than many of the high-tech yachts her grandfather detested. He could be brutal about his nod to craftsmanship, but this was a Burger, and all class. She was outfitted with light wood floors and walls, and large windows (not skimpy portholes) that gave a panoramic view of whatever port the *Balboa* might be docked in. Ellis could hardly believe their good fortune in being allowed to share the magnificent experience for even a few hours.

And she'd been thrilled when greeted by Chad's brother, Captain Matt, to find he was wearing his official outfit for the occasion: white fitted shirt with epaulets and the boat's insignia on the breast pocket; white slacks, and gray boat shoes. Even their Notary had worn a charming cocktail dress with a nautical flare since she would be standing near him for the mock ceremony.

"Isn't this grand," Hazel said as she walked on board.

"They've done us proud," Linden said. "Janet, watch your heels."

"Don't fuss, honey, I'm fine," Janet said. "You just pay attention to our girl over there and make sure you know what you're supposed to do at the ceremony."

"Yes dear."

"Millie, Fred, you both look fantastic," Linden said as he held out a hand to stabilize Fred on the boarding plank.

"You don't look so bad yourself," Fred said.

"Did you take your Dramamine, Fred?"

"Dad, that's not nice."

"Just havin' some fun sweetheart; Fred's known me for years, but I know he tends to get seasick."

"And you never let me forget it. Just like John."

"Here come Marilyn and Sheila." Ellis had personally called Marilyn with all the details and even offered to have Artie escort her to the party.

"Your pearls look lovely with that dress," Hazel said as

Marilyn stepped aboard. "And, you must be Sheila."

"Nice to meet you Mrs. Mowry."

"Hazel, please. Where's our groom, Ellis?"

"Making sure the champagne is ready; he wants to have a welcome toast once all the guests are here."

Jeanie moved in next to Ellis, and whispered, "I need you downstairs."

"Below, Jeanie."

"Whatever, just come."

At the bottom of the curved staircase, Jeanie turned and pointed to her back. "My zips stuck."

"Were you trying to take your dress off?"

"No, just trying to adjust my bra and now I can't get the damn thing back up."

"There you go." Ellis patted the top of the zipper. "You look great."

"I can't believe I wanted to wear these shoes; my feet are already killing me."

"Take them off, then, I don't mind."

"Chad needs to see me in this *whole* outfit."

"It's your call, and just so you know, he's up top with his brother, and he really looks in his element on a yacht."

"I don't know if I can take it."

"He came alone, so just be patient."

"Easy for you to say; your big guy nearly salivates every time he looks over at you in this skin-tight number."

"Couldn't have gotten into it without the low carb thing, but wait till he sees the little fake veil I have to put on when we practice our vows."

"Don't worry, he won't change his mind, but I'm happy to report I overheard his mother telling him that she was very proud and happy for him."

"How long were you going to wait to tell me that little tidbit?"

"I just did."

"God, you can be infuriating," Ellis said. "But let's get ourselves some champagne and you can finish telling me whatever else I need to know."

Music was coming from the internal speaker system on the aft deck and in the short time they'd been below deck, the party had magically gotten into full swing. Now that everyone was on one level, Ellis counted twenty-one heads. "What happened to the other two?"

"The flu."

"Mark's partner is really gorgeous," Ellis said. "Poor Cindy."

"How come you don't worry about me like that?"

"Because you will land on your feet like always; she on the other hand, is too shy to go after what she wants."

"What I want is about to make a toast; put your stupid veil on."

"Last chance you two," Chad said raising his glass.

"Give it up man; here's to the 28th," Artie said. "The celebration has officially begun."

"I can't believe this is all happening," Ellis said as she watched the little nibbles disappearing and the music shifting gears as glass after glass were raised on their behalf until Artie had to step in and introduce the Notary.

"I think I'm going to cry," Janet said.

"Can you at least wait till Saturday?" Linden said.

"Oh hush; I'll cry when I want."

"Children, please," Hazel said. "I can't hear what they're saying."

Everyone quieted down when the Notary held up her hand and began directing the wedding party as to how they were to stand and what she'd be saying once they were in their places on the lawn at the Colony. And, it was all going just fine until Chloe let out a small screech of pain.

"Oh, please god, not now!" Hazel said.

"False alarm, everyone!"

"I don't know who yelled that, but I'm really grateful we didn't have to call an ambulance," Janet said.

"They're just about wrapped up anyway," Linden said. "They've faked their vows and she's tossed the fake flowers and I'm hungry."

"Men!"

"Hang on there; you said I shouldn't eat before we

came and a man cannot go on booze alone."

"I'll go and see what I can round up for you, and that way I can make sure you eat something that won't give you gas all night long."

~

Hours later out on their own back deck, Artie said, "Quite a scare there for a moment."

"I almost peed my pants," Ellis said. "And yet, all I could think about was how wonderful it is that she's having a baby."

"You'll have one too; just not as painfully."

"How do you always manage to find the absolutely perfect thing to say to make me smile."

"That, my girl, is why you're marrying me."

"And that my guy, is why we're going to practice for our honeymoon, now!"

Chapter 30

In a room similar to the one she'd slept in only months before, Hazel Mowry pushed her gold rings over the knobs of her arthritic fingers, newly manicured in rose pink and visibly shaking. There was a lot at stake here today, the least of which was her own emotional revolving door. Once again it was that old expectation versus disappointment doing battle as if she'd never learned her lesson. The bedside clock said 1:14, cold blue numbers in a white plastic case, harsh, but more tolerable this time around than it had been three months earlier. And since her dress was ruched, and wrinkle free, she had dressed in the comfort of her own bedroom in hopes that doing so would offset the case of nerves which had begun the night before. The sapphire blue was meant to enhance her eyes, which suddenly appeared like jewels—even with the creases surrounding them—creating a certain je ne sais quoi quality to her appearance. All her efforts on Ellis's behalf were going to play out on this beautiful day, which even the trained forecasters had never seen coming. Hazel had done her best to make peace with the fact that there had been no reply from Eduardo for whatever reason:

perhaps he was infirm, possibly he had no interest in memories as old as theirs, or he too found his appearance not up to snuff to go chasing after an old dream. And, admittedly, she'd come to loathe the sound that so many years piled one on top of another made. A layer cake of life, she'd thought and maybe Eduardo was no longer interested in slicing open such a dry dessert. Of course, there was the awful chance that some terrible condition like dementia had obliterated those beautiful days and nights, which in her mind would be crueler than if he simply chose not to see her again.

There was a soft knock at her door, a reverie buster that had come at just the right moment. She opened it to find Ellis standing there with her frilly white lingerie peeking out from a floral dressing gown. "Thank you for letting me borrow this, Gran."

"It looks perfect on you; and what is your mother up to over there?"

"She's trying to hang my gown on that hook so it won't get mussed up before the ceremony. We're just playing around with make-up, but we want you to be in there with us."

"I'll be just a minute."

Hazel ducked back into her room, feeling like she'd opened a time capsule instead of her door. Had she been asked, she probably could have written the entire script for the day, except for the ending.

Janet's real beauty had been late in coming, but there was no doubt her daughter once dressed in the right colors and perfectly made up, looked almost exotic today. There was no denying it now.

Hazel thought of their entourage that morning, the entire wedding party with the exception of Chloe, dashing through the hotel like school children let out on recess, giggling and rushing outside to the pool deck. Chloe had started carrying the baby low now, but she'd been assured she still had weeks to go, and Hazel had sent up a prayer to Sloane to watch over this day. Who else would Hazel even consider praying to while standing in the lobby of the Colony Hotel?

"Gran, what're you waiting for?" Ellis called from behind the door.

"I'm coming, I'm coming," Hazel said as she stepped into the hall.

"Peter's waiting in there, and I want you in those pictures."

Hazel walked down the hallway and ran her hand over the wainscoting and stared at the dress on the hanger in front of the tall window that framed the sun. *It's still Maine, so we'll see.*

"Hi Mrs. Mowry."

"Lovely to see you again, Peter. You have a beautiful

day to work."

"I'm a lucky guy to be able to do what I love."

"Well, it's a great day for a wedding," Hazel said.

"There's some great shots from the *Balboa* that I think she'll like to include in her album."

"Great party the other night, Mrs. M," Jeanie called out.

"I thought so too, Jeanie; Chad's quite a guy."

"Isn't he," Jeanie said.

"Sorry I gave everybody a scare," Chloe said. "Little Kenny just won't stop kicking."

"Janet was like that."

"You never told me," Janet piped in.

"I thought your grandmother Midge told you when you were pregnant with Jake, but then my memory gets a little muddled these days."

"Wouldn't she have loved all this?" Janet said swinging her arms out.

"Hard to know; she was full of surprises. But I know she would have been very, very proud."

Even as she was talking with the girls, Hazel watched Peter go through the motions and realized she'd already started gazing through another lens: Sloane sitting where Ellis was, at the foot of the bed with Jeanie applying her eye makeup; Mrs. Harmon where Janet was standing, holding onto the veil for safe keeping. And, without realizing in those hours before the wedding, that it would be Eduardo with his clumsy camera who would be looking upon her with any interest at all. Hazel hadn't even known his name at that hour and not even when he'd made her blush that first time.

Someone brought up a tray with small sandwiches and a bottle of champagne. Hazel watched from across the room as Jeanie filled each flute and handed them out, making sure there was a juice for Chloe and giving the last one to Hazel. "Here's to the girls in blue," Jeanie said.

"To the girls," Hazel said choking up. "May they always be watching."

Ellis didn't care that Peter, with his fine digital instrument and extra lenses, was snapping away, snaring every tear from every crying eye. And though she couldn't imagine what miracles he'd produce for the end product or how much he would capture that would be treasured to the degree of Sloane's, Ellis knew there wouldn't be any of this without her grandmother. "Oh, Gran, please don't tear up now; this is such a special day for both of us, and none of it would have been possible without you."

"You are deserving of every ounce of happiness you can squeeze out of this life, and don't you ever forget it!"

Clapping her hands and brushing away one of the many tears she would shed this day, Janet said, "Ladies, time to get dressed. "Peter, I think you can step out now and meet us at the bottom of the stairs."

"You remembered," Hazel said.

"Engrained on my brain since childhood. This was what I'd hoped for our girl the first time, but we have a chance now to do it up right as you've always pointed out."

"She's a gorgeous bride, and you my dear daughter, look fabulous."

"I've lost five pounds and the flushing seems to have slowed down, and it's been fun listening to Marilyn complain about hers."

"Where is she by the way?"

"Keeping the boys on track; said she needed to have a talk with her son."

"I'm starting to get butterflies myself; how about I meet you all downstairs too?"

"You know what to tell Peter; after all, you were the one at the top of the stairs."

Hazel smiled and left the room feeling a little less grandmotherly than when she'd gone in. She walked past the tall window in the hall, and suddenly sucked in her breath. The light had fallen on the unusual ruching making the deep blue material sparkle like the sea beyond, and she all but glided down the stairs to find the rest of their party.

Chapter 31

Once downstairs, she had a brief and pleasant exchange with Peter, liking him more and more for his insight into the unique qualities of the hotel and the natural lighting it offered. And much to her surprise, he said he was grateful that Ellis had sought him out that day. It had been, he'd added, quite a bumpy road back to recovery. After that and with time on her hands, and since for the first time in modern history—as her granddaughter had pointed out— Hazel would not have to be changing *her* clothes, she could poke around. She was just beginning to relax when she spotted Millie walking toward her.

"Are you terribly disappointed?"

"I'm okay actually. I really didn't think he'd reply and today is all about Ellis, and I'm so fortunate to be able to take part in all this."

"You couldn't have asked for a better day; Fred's even talking about coming back sometime, maybe for an anniversary."

"I'm glad he decided to say yes," Hazel said. "Have you been out to see where they're holding the ceremony?"

"We walked out there earlier with the Notary; it's such

a glorious spot."

"I keep thinking that John is looking down at his angel and if he is, I hope he's watching out for Jake too."

"I didn't dare bring up his name or Janet would have just dissolved—Linden told me they hadn't heard from him in over two weeks."

"I'd give anything if these damn conflicts would end!"

"Don't get me started, or you and I will end up very drunk at the end of this day."

"Then let's just saunter down to the ballroom so I can take a look at what they've done with my money."

"I've requested lobster, so thank you in advance."

"Like you don't get enough at Robinson's?"

"What can I say, I'm addicted."

"I almost forgot to tell you how wonderful you look in lavender, and I don't know why you never wear it."

"My mother always told me it made my skin look gray."

"Why did we think our mothers knew best? Just think of all the times Midge told me I shouldn't wear pink or not to go in swimming after I ate, among so many other backwater ideas."

"Too late now; they're gone and we're here trying to do the best we can, and speaking of best, will you look at this room."

Hazel hardly recognized it. True to her many gifts, Lara

had given Ellis that elusive theme she'd been hoping for, and had transformed the ballroom into a summer garden. Small potted trees enhanced by blue and white ribbons had been placed strategically near the tables: rounds that would seat as many as six and one long table for the wedding party, skipping the sweetheart table altogether. Ellis had been right to go along with the blue-themed vases and white flowers and now they were everywhere except for the centerpieces, for which Ellis and Lara had chosen highball glasses in sets of three and filled them with unscented blue irises cut to size and formed into small clusters, making it easier for the guests to converse without craning their necks. The little gift boxes Ellis had found were on the side of each place setting. Polished flatware gleamed from the folds of large white napkins.

A long table covered with a white tablecloth was already topped with stemmed glasses and bottles of wine. Hazel thought she'd walked into the photograph from Sloane's wedding when she saw where the table had been placed and with one of the hotel bartenders officiating over a tub of cold beer, just in case one of the 'boys' needed a little hair of the dog.

"Don't you just love the sound of corks popping?" Millie said. "I'd get married all over again if I could do it here."

"Not me; I don't want to get married again."

"Are you just saying that because you're disappointed?"

"I don't think I'm marriage material anymore, that's all."

"Nonsense."

"No really; I think I'm too set in my ways now, and even if Eduardo would have turned up, I wasn't looking for that to happen."

"Just don't go closing your mind off to possibilities, okay."

"OKAY."

"Now, let's go and see if we can find the chef so we can sample what else you've paid for."

"I feel like you've just been let out," Hazel said.

"In a way I have; I don't have to cook all weekend."

~

An hour later, all the wedding guests were gathered on the back lawn. Hazel sensed tears building once again as she spotted two little girls peeking out from behind a nearby bush to get a glimpse of the bride who truth be told, looked very much like a fairy princess as she made her way along the stone path. For all of Marilyn's concerns, Ellis's gown looked struck by sunbeams, allowing the whiteness to take on an ethereal quality.

302

Hazel's breath caught as Linden slowed down next to her. Ellis shifted her bouquet and with her free hand she touched the pendant and blew Hazel a kiss. As she returned the gesture, Hazel caught Linden swiping his eyes as if trying to shoo away a bug. Suddenly, Janet, who'd been up front waiting for Linden to place Ellis's hand in Artie's and then join her in the front row, let out a high-pitched, hiccup-like sob straight out of the wedding scene in the movie, *The Birdcage*. John had loved it as well as the original farce known as *Le Cage aux Folles*. Hazel looked at her daughter and beamed and then rolled her eyes heavenward.

It was a simple, sweet ceremony that even without an altar to stand at or a pergola to kiss under, the bride and groom couldn't have been more in love or have written their scene any better. And once they'd been officially pronounced man and wife, Artie swooped Ellis into his arms, let out a whoop and dipped her in a way no one saw coming and kissed her in a way that Hazel was certain Ellis would never forget.

Jeanie squealed and Chloe grimaced and patted her tummy and as soon as she gave the all-clear, everyone let out a collective sigh and the entire crowd cheered and shouted. Then birdseed was tossed—better for the planet—according to one of the guests standing close to Hazel.

During it all, Peter had kept roving, taking what he needed from each precious hug or kiss or utilizing the backdrop as Ellis had instructed.

Hazel had another of her déjà vu moments as she watched him doing what he did so well, again stifling tears before she would have to redo her makeup. Then he began rounding everyone up for the one photograph that would take centerstage on all their walls or side tables for a very long time, and Hazel quickly pulled a tissue from her sleeve. She hung back, needing to watch from inside the hotel as he put everyone into their places; there was no point in ignoring what was flowing through her body and mind at this moment, but she needed to compose herself before becoming part of the group. She'd had a brief conversation earlier with Ellis and had emphasized that she didn't intend to be in all the photos anyway.

Once inside and from her place behind the windows, Hazel was free to imagine Sloane and their October day. Hazel knew she'd already gotten her money's worth and knew that she'd most likely never be here again. And from this position, she was able to frame her own legacy, the family she and John had nurtured and loved. And for the first time in a long time, she really missed Midge's presence.

Outside, the bridal party was doing their best to stand still, but it was nearly impossible with men like Artie and

Chad leading the pack. Hazel couldn't be certain, but she thought she saw Chad look at Jeanie as if he'd never quite seen her before. Weddings could do that to people, Hazel thought as she saw Jeanie return the look with a wink and a blush.

This wedding day had a few more pluses. It had been gifted by a light breeze with a calm ocean in the background. There'd be no hair disasters or uplifted skirts for this gang to worry about. And though they were all older than those in Sloane's wedding party, they still had the impish expressions and unformed facial contours of their school photographs, and resembled many of the parents Hazel knew through Janet.

The groomsmen didn't wear their hair as long as those of her youth, more like what Jake's would look like if he'd been here, and then she had to force herself to stop playing that mind game or she'd drive herself crazy. *Maybe you should have called the Pentagon after all.*

But for all their difference, the young men standing outside still managed to mug for the camera until the very last moment when Hazel realized that Peter was much smoother at getting his way than Eduardo had been. But then, as she already pointed out to her granddaughter, photography hadn't been his first love.

You're about to lose it old girl, she thought as she felt a soft shudder go through her chest wall — the tears she had successfully held at bay for the last hour were about to consume her. But they wouldn't be tears of joy as most people would think if she finally broke down. She had lied to Millie; she was so disappointed. She dabbed her eyes and saw Midge's face reflected in the window doing the same, and Hazel realized right then and there, that she had learned nothing about expectations after all. She heard footsteps and put on a false smile before turning around.

"There you are, Mom, we're all waiting on you."

Outside, a big cloud scudded by as Hazel took her place next to Janet. She and Linden would flank Ellis's right side with Marilyn and Sheila to Artie's left, and for a moment the group was in the cloud's shadow, leaving Peter to rethink their position. Hazel took advantage of the moment, sucking in her disappointment to paste on the type of smile that she hoped would endear her family to her in years to come. Then, the cloud gave way and the sun touched the variegated layers of the bridesmaids' dresses and glinted against Hazel's sheath, and she no longer had to fake the smile. By the time Peter had finished, it was four o'clock and everyone was more than ready to party.

"Gran, come with me for a minute, please."

"What's up baby?"

"I just wanted you to know I'm sorry I got your hopes up; he doesn't deserve a woman like you anyway."

"Oh, Ellis, you didn't do anything wrong. It just wasn't meant to be."

"Maybe, but I wanted so badly for it to happen."

Not as much as me, Hazel thought. "I'm fine, but I am hungry; shall we go and enjoy what their marvelous chef has created. Millie and I had a sample earlier."

Ellis linked arms with her grandmother and said, "May you forever reign, Hazel Mowry!"

Chapter 32

Inside the ballroom, the shining crystal shimmered over a sea of blue, and the photographs that Peter would take here, would forever memorialize the heart and spirit of Boothbay Harbor's finest, at least in Hazel's mind. One really could go home again in every sense but one, Hazel thought, but pride never went out of fashion, and for a moment she wondered if that had been one of Mother Mowry's quotes.

For a little while it looked like the guests were playing a game of musical chairs as they sat down and got back up again only to move nearer to someone they hadn't seen in ages. Place cards were moved around and no one seemed to mind. And if anyone noticed the difference, they were quickly caught up in the toasts as the sound of clinking silverware rang through the room. The bride and groom kissed on cue and Hazel cast a loving eye on the newlyweds and tried to remember if that little ritual had been around in the '60s. She and Millie and Fred had perfect seats to watch and hear without difficulty, and as Fred pointed out when Millie sent out a cheer, no one had to shout.

Toasts were made and food was served, and with each new course, a cheer went up. And even the silly little intermezzo was scarfed down without comment from the head table. This group could eat, Hazel thought as she watched from just feet away. The din inside the room rose and fell according to the number of plates coming and going until it was finally time for the cake.

Hazel thought of the monster cake for Sloane's wedding as she watched a waitress roll out a stand with a tastefully sized cake with a most unusual waterfall design, and just as the girl put the stand in place, a drumroll came from the far side of the ballroom, and the musicians walked in carrying their instruments: the band from Boston Hazel had heard so much about. Chad clapped Artie on the back and Ellis clapped her hands together like a surprised little girl. Hazel immediately realized that Ellis hadn't for once believed they'd actually turn up.

Artie stood and took Ellis's hand and walked her toward the cake.

"Are you okay, Hazel?"

"Just remembering, Millie, not to worry." Hazel was remembering every detail now; the way Mike had taken a huge hunk of cake and pushed it into Sloane's mouth and everyone laughing because that was the way it had always been done. And then, bringing her out of one of her many reveries, Hazel heard the fanfare change to something far more melodic, something even Artie would be able to follow. Taking Ellis's hand, he led her to the opening in the dancefloor forcing those who'd moved in to take photos, to step aside. Everyone wanted a glimpse of this first dance, and Marilyn had pulled out her own camera along with so many other guests. Of course, she would be up there soon dancing with her son, and Hazel wanted that to be a moving moment to remember and not a tug of war between the Glover women.

Artie had no sooner managed the perfect twirl when Linden stepped in to dance with his daughter, at last. Hazel thought her face might crumple as she was reminded of the picture in her album of the little tot on Eduardo's toes. She was beginning to succumb to so much of what needed to be put behind her, and there were still hours to be filled before she could realistically exit the party.

"They're awfully good," Millie said. "Fred give Hazel a turn around the floor."

"I thought you'd never ask," Fred said.

"You don't have to bother, really."

"It'd be my pleasure, Hazel."

They waltzed around for a few minutes, passing Artie with his mother, and before Hazel could suggest they return to their seats, Artie switched partners, taking her away from Fred. "You have to do me the honor too, *Gran.*"

"I like the sound of that, Artie, and I hope with all my heart that you and Ellis will have a long and happy marriage."

"I love her to death."

"It shows, believe me." Hazel motioned toward her table where Millie was leaning in toward Fred, and said, "How about you maneuver us back to my table before my friends get up to no good."

Hazel sat back and watched as Millie and Fred took another twirl around the floor. Janet had just walked away and was headed over to join Linden at the bar. It was a little like watching sports, Hazel thought as her head swiveled this way and that across the dancefloor.

Hazel suddenly craved a glass of champagne. The one used for the toast was adequate, but now she wanted the one they'd had that morning, the expensive one with overtones of some grape she hadn't remembered. "Something to inspire," she said as she walked up to the bartender and pointed to one of the champagne glasses. He grabbed a bottle from under the table. "Is this what you're looking for?"

"Perfect." Hazel accepted the glass of champagne, but the minute she began to drink, bubbles went up her nose and she sneezed.

"Bless you," Marilyn said coming up behind Hazel.

"Thanks, want to join me?"

"You bet I would. It isn't every day you watch your only boy get married."

"How fortunate we are that he's here and not somewhere overseas."

"Oh, Hazel, I'm sorry, that was tasteless of me."

"Not at all; it's just that Jake's been on my mind a lot today."

"Let's drink to Jake then and fair winds and a following sea," Marilyn said. "Wasn't your John a seaman?"

"A perfect toast, and to new friendships," Hazel said raising her glass and clinking it against Marilyn's.

"I really envy Ellis those pearls you gave her."

"Speaking of, what's this I heard about a certain visit to a certain doctor?"

"Lordy, don't tell me it's all over town. It was meant as a joke, but between us girls, he was a real heart-stopper."

"What did you think of Captain Matt the other night?"

"Can you keep a secret?"

"I do believe I can."

"He asked me out for Tuesday night."

"See, your world has already opened up…a new mahjong partner, a prospective beau in the offing, who knows, maybe the doc will remember your name, or at least those fabulous pearls."

"You're a lot different than I thought when I first met you, Hazel Mowry, and I'm truly glad."

"Same here, Marilyn Glover, same here."

~

"Did I see you and my new mother-in-law making nice over there?" Ellis bent over Hazel's chair and whispered, "Artie and I have a little secret and we want you to be the first to know."

"You're pregnant!"

"No, but we are going to begin adoption proceedings as soon as we come back from Monhegan, and then we'll sit everyone down and work through what we've learned from our attorney."

"You're working with Jim Bensen, right?"

"Yes, just like you and grandad and the Mowrys before."

"Is he that old?"

"His son is about to take over, so I'm not really too concerned about that, but we need to put the wheels in motion now."

"I'm thrilled, and I know both families will be, and I promise, mum's the word," Hazel said. "Now go on, finish making your rounds."

The band had gone through a number of oldies, appealing to Hazel's generation of which there were very few in sight at the moment. Then the musicians worked their way through some of the more well-known show tunes while Hazel's eyes glazed over. When they took another break, she went into the powder room off the ballroom and patted cold water on her eyes and refreshed her makeup and stretched her arms over her head to loosen her back. The hotel had provided ambiance, great food, a wonderful staff, and not very comfortable chairs.

By the time she walked out, another set was being played and this time it was a deep melody that might have been a prelude to a love song. Perhaps the bride and groom were going to take another turn on the dancefloor, she thought craning her head around a pair of broad shoulders.

Sure enough, there were Ellis and Artie, cheek to cheek in a modest slow dance that made Artie look at least semi-comfortable. Hazel walked along the border and made it to her table only to notice that Millie and Fred had gone over to dance alongside the bride and groom.

Hazel sat down, relieved, and yet wistful. She saw Millie tap Ellis on the shoulder, bringing Ellis out of her blissful trance, and Hazel suddenly fastened on their exchange. Ellis's eyes opened wide and they both looked over at Hazel. There was this funny volley going on: Ellis's lips had formed a small o and she looked in the other direction at her mother, who was oblivious to everything but the music. Hazel kept watching, thinking Janet needed attention, but then there was another exchange of glances, and Ellis had become laser-focused on the outer edge of the dancefloor nearest the doorway.

From her seat, Hazel could only make out the top of a silvery head of hair, and then she watched as a not very tall man emerged whole, his smile unreadable and his stride easy and purposeful. There was strength in his stubbled jawline. Her eyes took him in from head to toe: the thick, wavy hair, a casual linen jacket paired with a white shirt, and dark trousers, and eyes that roamed the room with calm, determined intention. Hazel was as becalmed as a sailboat without wind. There were no words left, no tears either, nothing to spoil what she actually thought she was imagining: a somewhat different version of the man whose memories she'd clung to. He stopped just short of her chair and as he brushed away some of his unruly hair, she felt her lips opening into an o that would be seen across the room.

"Is it really you?"

"I hope so."

"I didn't think you'd come."

"Are you okay that I did?"

"I don't know."

"Should I leave?"

"No… but why did you come?" She wanted to hear her name, like the way she always heard it in her head, not the one she'd learned to live with, so she waited.

"Hazel…we're never too old to dance."

Acknowledgements

I love weddings, and once upon a time I was one of the 'girls in blue taffeta', but it wasn't until a visit to the Colony Hotel that I'd ever considered actually writing about weddings. At the time I was researching the Dunton/Ellis branches of my family tree and was focused on the idea of historical fiction. But the wedding characters kept drawing me back, and before I knew it, Hazel Mowry was taking center stage.

During the years it took to write this novel, Hazel evolved into the matriarch of her clan just as the women of my own had been doing for decades here in Maine. My research also turned up June Patten Webster, aka June Campbell Rose, as a fourth cousin. I'm so grateful she allowed me to cast her rightful place in the story. I must also acknowledge the Failing/Corbishley families from New York state, for without their enthusiasm there might not have been Boothbay Harbor bookseller, Chad Corbishley.

A big shout out to the staff and volunteers at the Boothbay Harbor Memorial Library for their continuing support and assistance. And also, my thanks to a wonderful group of

Maine women who have given of their time as beta readers and as my support team: Ruth Alley, Hilary Bartlett, Melanie Howe, Lynne Nicoletta, Ann Sutter, and Meg Donaldson.

Last but not least is my editor, Joan Dempsey, who after getting me past the inevitable rewrites, always gives me the courage to fly on my own.

~

About the Author

Cheryl Blaydon is the author of the novels *The Memory Keepers, Island Odyssey, The Heart of Stone,* and *Beyond the Ledge.* She lives in East Boothbay, Maine.

www.cherylblaydon.com

CPSIA information can be obtained
at www.ICGtesting.com
Printed in the USA
FSHW012356230420
69448FS